A Prayer For Life

When he recovered consciousness he found himself on the couch along the wall where the light from the door fell. Either his body was bound so tightly that he could scarcely breathe or the excruciating agony made it feel so. Matt Taylor knelt beside him, feeling his pulse.

"Dick," he said hoarsely. "I reckon you'll die—pronto."

Richard's lips framed an almost inaudible "No!"

"Your arm's gone—shoulder—top of your lung! Man, tell me what to do when—when—"

"Matt . . . I'll . . . not die."

"I hope not. But I reckon you will. Did all I could, Dick. Listen, man! What'll I tell—do? . . . I trailed you—found your gun. It hadn't been fired!"

"Tell . . . do . . . nothing."

"Ahuh!" The Mormon's dark and grim glance rested wonderingly upon Richard. "Shall I pray for you?"

"Yes . . . that . . . I live."

This religious Mormon bowed his head over Richard and prayed in husky fervid whisper, the last of which grew intelligible: "And damn their cursed souls to hell!"

Other books by Zane Grey:

Yaqui and Other Indian Stories

The Big Land

Last of the Plainsmen

The Westerner

Shark

Savage Kingdom

The Last Ranger

Buffalo Hunter

Spirit of the Border

The Last Trail

We will send you a free catalog on request. Any titles not in your local bookstore can be purchased by mail. Send the price of the book plus 50¢ shipping charge to Tower Books, P.O. Box 511, Murray Hill Station, New York, N.Y. 10156-0511.

Titles currently in print are available for industrial and sales promotion at reduced rates. Address inquiries to Tower Publications, Inc., Two Park Avenue, New York, N.Y. 10016, Attention: Premium Sales Department.

TENDERFOOT

Zane Grey

TOWER BOOKS 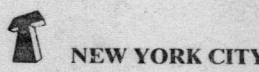 NEW YORK CITY

A TOWER BOOK

Published by

Tower Publications, Inc.
Two Park Avenue
New York, N.Y. 10016

Copyright © MCMLXXVII by Zane Grey, Inc.

All rights reserved
Printed in the United States

TENDERFOOT

When Zane Grey died in 1939, he left numerous books and stories unfinished. Over the years his heirs have made some of these fragments available for publication in the interest of satisfying the great demand for stories by the most famous of Western writers. We are proud to present this recently discovered fragment by the incomparable Zane Grey.

I

Young Ernest Selby had inherited the Red Rock Ranch in Arizona, but before he took possession he wanted to find out why the ranch had been losing money for three years. He decided to pose as a cowboy and sign on as a hand at Red Rock even though he was a tenderfoot and not even a Westerner. When he had learned all there was to know, he would reveal his true identity and take control of his ranch.

Ernest went to Red Rock and called himself Ernest Howard. There he found out that Hepford, the ranch manager, had been juggling the finances to profit himself . . . and to Ernest's surprise, he also found himself falling in love with Hepford's beautiful daughter, Anne. But Anne acted like a flirt, dividing her attentions between Ernest and Hepford's crony, Hyslip. Hyslip was a skylarking dude who liked the ladies, and Ernest's best friend, Nebraskie, threatened violence if Hyslip didn't stay away from Nebraskie's girl.

All in all, the tenderfoot from Iowa got a lot more than he bargained for in the West—especially one night when he broke into Hepford's house and found himself trapped in Anne's bedroom . . .

Ernest made a sharp gesture, which ended with his fingers to his lips. But that did not prevent

Anne from crying out: "Ernest!" He made a hissing sound as he whispered to her to keep still.

"What does this mean!" she exclaimed, her look of surprise turning into anger and indignation.

He advanced with long strides, to halt at the foot of her bed. Here the lamplight shone full on him. Anne's big eyes widened as they swept from his bare head to his stocking feet, his menacing posture, his gun. She sank back with a gasp.

"In God's name! What're you doing in my room? What are you going to do to me?"

"That depends," he replied, very low and fiercely.

She sat up again, her red hair tumbling around her white face and bare shoulders. Her terror, her agitation, tended to make her appear more beautiful than Ernest had ever seen her. It occurred to him that his sudden entrance and his attitude might well have made her think he had broken in to her bedroom to revenge himself upon her for her cruelty to him.

"Ernest—you—you wouldn't" she began, and lifted a shaking hand.

"I'd do anything, Anne Hepford," he whispered threateningly, bending over the bed, fixing her with his eyes. He meant to frighten her until she helped him out of his dilemma. "You made me love you to distraction. Then you betrayed me— scorned me before your father—and that damned blackguard!" he whispered hoarsely.

"Oh, but wait—listen. Ernest," she begged wildly. "I'm not so vile as you think. When we got back from that ride we took everybody ridiculed me. I was furious anyhow—because I—I began to see I really cared. I wouldn't give in to it. I encouraged Hyslip again. And when I saw you at Brooks; I wanted to make you feel as miserable as I was. . . . But I was sorry. That settled me. Tonight I wrote you—telling how wrong I was to hurt you—how sorry I was that I had done all this to you. You must believe me, Ernest."

"Anne Hepford, you're lying," he retorted, not needing now to feign anger.

"No, Ernest. I've got the letter under my pillow." She turned and, tumbling the pillows, extracted a letter which she held out.

The intruder eagerly leaned over the bed to snatch the letter from her fingers. A glance showed that it was addressed to him. The envelope was thick, and undoubtedly its contents occupied many pages. Slowly he dropped the missive into his pocket. His doubt of her remained as great as all the pain she had caused him. He willed himself to not yield to her charm, to her lies, only to be humiliated all over again. Yet the sweet loveliness of her, as she lay helpless there in bed, made him catch his breath.

"So you've taken to writing letters now? Why don't you get the Dude to deliver them for you?" he asked harshly.

"Oh, please, Ernest," she pleaded. "I know I deserve—oh, Ernest, I've been heartless. But I know how wrong I was. I don't ask you to forgive me—just to believe me. It's all in that letter. I confessed. I told the truth at last—how I found out that I really cared for you—hated myself for my blindness, my stubbornness—begged you to understand—asked you to come back to Red Rock and I'd make everything all right."

"Anne, what you say is impossible."

"Indeed it's not. It's all in that letter—and if you just cain't believe me, read it heah and now. I don't blame you. I—I've been a liar—a flirt—a cat—a coward. But, Ernest, I didn't know myself—I didn't."

"If it's true—it's too late!" he said, turning away in order that she might not see his face.

She sat up, and reaching for her dressing gown, she slipped the coverlet back and moved to the foot of the bed. Her glance fell to the floor. She was flushing scarlet now.

"Not too late, Ernest. Oh, don't say that—not if you still—"

Heavy footsteps and a knocking on the door silenced her. Ernest drew back. He suddenly realized what an awkward position he was in, and what a compromising situation it must be for the girl.

"Anne, are you awake?" called her father's voice.

"Oh, that you, Dad? Yes, I'm awake, but I'm in bed," she replied in tones that sounded unnatural to Ernest.

"Let me in."

It was then a subtle change passed over her. The startled look left her eyes.

"But, Dad, I told you. I'm in bed. I don't want to get up."

"Reckon you needn't. You have that money

safe?"

"Yes. I hid it away."

"All right. Never mind now. I'll probably be out all night . . . Anne, somethin' terrible's happened."

"What?"

"Young Howard killed Hyslip . . . the cowboys think it was murder."

Anne's horrified gaze transfixed him. "Oh, Dad—how awful!" she cried huskily.

"Wal, it was awful fer Hyslip an' it'll be awful fer Howard if we catch him," responded Hepford grimly. "It'll mean a lynchin'. I'm sorry to have to tell you, Anne. But you had somethin' to do with it. I told you to let that tenderfoot alone. I sensed that he was different from the start. Not a cowboy at all, not even a Westerner. He was out of his haid over you . . . But no use to rail. It's too late now. Let this be a lesson to you. Go to sleep, if you can. I'll tell you eyerythin' tomorrow."

He ceased and his heavy footsteps sounded down the hall. Voices came from the porch. There were others outside.

Ernest's heart, which had been in his throat, resumed its natural position. His consternation and then terror had all been for Nebraskie. In a flash he realized what had happened. Hepford and Hyslip had not gone to town. No doubt Hyslip had returned instead to Brooks' ranch, there to run into Nebraskie. Then in some way Hepford, and perhaps others, deliberately had mixed up Ernest's name in the case.

All of a sudden Ernest became aware of Anne.

While those thoughts had flashed through his mind he had forgotten her and where he was. She came sliding unsteadily along the bed, and reaching the footboard she raised herself to her knees and clasped Ernest with nerveless hands. Her face was ghastly white, her eyes were strained and full of dark terror.

"Oh, my God, I know now—why you said it's too late," she moaned. "I drove you to do it. I don't blame you. *I'm* to blame. Oh, Ernest why, why didn't you wait? Why didn't you come to me sooner? I can see it all now. Hyslip crowed over you. Aboot me! The damed conceited fool! And you killed him! Oh, may God forgive me."

Ernest put his arms around her and held her close, doubting his own senses. But he could feel her throbbing heart; he could see the tragic despair in her great eyes.

"Anne, hush. Your father—or someone else may hear you. My life is in danger," he whispered. "You heard what he said about a lynching."

"Yes—yes." She clung to him then, straining and trembling and shivering as with a chill. It was on Ernest's lips to tell her that he had not killed Hyslip, to assure her of his innocence, but he was powerless to resist the moment. What more would she say? What would she do? Again, he was finding himself convinced that in spite of all that had happened, this beautiful girl truly loved him. It seemed preposterous, incomprehensible, yet she might. She might prove it in some glorious way.

She drew back from him a little, and he could see her gathering her courage.

12

"We must leave Red Rock at once," she whispered.

"You would go with me?"

"Heaven help us. Yes, I'll go. Once across the territory line you'll be safe. But if you're caught now—Dad and his outfit will hang you. Oh, they hate you, Ernest, for some reason I can't figure out . . . We must go at once."

"Anne, you'd really—run off with me?" he asked wonderingly.

"I told you. Yes, yes. I will. I must. I'd never let you go alone."

"But why?"

"Because I've ruined you . . . And because I—I love you, Ernest." She put her arms around his neck and kissed him.

"But Anne. Think. Don't take a step like this—just out of remorse or sense of pity. You'd have to marry me."

"I'd want to, of course, Ernest. But I'll go whether you marry me or not. I'll give my life. I'll pay. I'm a new Anne Hepford. And I know what I'm doing. You killed a man because of me. But he deserved to die. I want you to live—for me."

"We'd be very poor, Anne. You've been used to everything you wanted. If you do this rash thing and afterward regret it—"

"I ask only to get you away from them . . . Ernest, you do love me still? I didn't make you despise me?"

No dream of love he had ever had could equal the sweetness and passion of her voice, the entreaty in her face.

"Anne, I love you more madly than ever. Still, I beg you once again. Think of what you're doing."

"Kiss me," she whispered, holding onto him. Her lips clung to his. Then with a quick movement she broke from him.

"I'll let you out this window," she said swiftly. "Keep in the dark. Find your shoes. I'll dress, pack a few things and meet you in fifteen minutes. Let's see. I'll go through the grove, down by the road. Wait for me near the big pine. I must try to get horses, if I can."

She turned down the lamp till the room was almost dark. Then she slid up the blind. The window was open. All appeared dark and quiet outside. "Now," she whispered, "and for my sake don't let anyone see you."

Without a word more Ernest slipped out, while she knelt to help him, clasp him, and kiss him once more. As her lips left his cheek they formed the word: "Darling." Then her hold loosened. Ernest dropped to the soft turf. The dim light from the window vanished.

He stood there for an instant like a man in a trance. How dark the night. How still! He was trembling all over. He listened. The sound of faint hoof beats came to his listening ears. Stealthily he moved, making no sound. He parted the leaves of the shrubbery and moved noiselessly through them, away from the house, into the grove. He found his shoes and put them on. He had to feel for the trunks of the pines. One by one he passed through them, gradually gaining control over his faculties, as he crept toward the road. At the edge of the grove he stopped to make sure of his further course. He knew the way as well as if it had been daylight. Across the open to the left several of the bunkhouses showed lights from their windows. He crossed the wide dark space to the right of the grove, and gained the high vine-covered fence. He slipped along this to the end, where it turned at right angles, forming one side of the barnyard. He had only to go round the barn to the lane. Then as he listened the sound of hoofs came again, louder now, followed by the crunch of wheels on gravel. Someone was bringing the buckboard from the house. It was coming too slowly to be driven. Suddenly the sounds were drowned by the rush of horses from the other direction. Several riders galloped by, toward the ranch house. Ernest saw the dark forms.

He did not have a great while to think and plan. Absolutely, beyond any equivocation he would take Anne at her word, elope with her, marry her, and let the rest take care of itself. Exultation swelled in his heart. But they could not walk. He must procure horses. Perhaps it would not be the best course to wait until Anne joined him. Nevertheless he waited. Soon in the gloom dim forms appeared—Pedro leading the team, still hitched to the buckboard. The Mexican lad was humming a tune. He went by, continuing on into the barnyard.

Ernest took advantage of his opportunity, and passing the barn, hurried down the lane. The customary quiet of the ranch at this hour appeared to have been disrupted. The sound of distant voices came to his ear and the pounding of boots on wooden floors. The cowboys were moving to and fro. Ernest worried about the three horsemen who had passed. He wished they would return. However, he reflected, they could have gone on toward Springertown.

He did not proceed more than halfway to the big pine that stood close to the road, but waited just out of sight of the barn, and listened with all his might, peering impatiently into the gloom. He was sure Anne would come. He had dispelled his last doubt of her. And he thanked God that his faith had persisted, despite all appearances, despite his own weak pretenses up to the very end. Yet how wrong he had been that day at Brooks' farm. She had only been distraught. Her vanity and her pride had succumbed to her love for a tenderfoot masquerading as a penniless cowboy. Ernest blessed the deception he had practiced. Otherwise he might never have won her. It had taken the tragedy of Hyslip's killing to make a woman of her.

Suddenly his keen ear caught the sound of light swift steps. His blood raced. She was coming. Sure as the stars shone she was coming to meet him, to go away with him, to share what she thought would be his vicissitudes. Then a dark flitting shadow emerged from the gloom. He waited until he recognized it. She wore a black coat and carried a small bag. Ernest stepped out from his hiding place. She shied like a frightened colt. Then he spoke her name softly, reassuring her. Joining her, he took her bag.

"I'm late. But I had—some narrow—escapes," she whispered, her breath coming in little gasps. "I got out easy enough. Dad has men there. I—I listened a moment—at my door . . . Now, we must have horses."

"Pedro just led the buckboard into the barnyard," said Ernest.

"Good, I'll get it. Wait at the gate for me. Have it open." She was gone before Ernest had a reply ready. He obeyed her, hurrying down the lane. She could do anything with Pedro, or any of the other hired hands for that matter. Before he reached the gate he heard the buckboard coming, the horses at a brisk trot. Ernest ran to open the gate.

The black team approached almost to where he stood. Anne slowed up, but did not stop. "Jump in!" she shouted, with an excited little laugh. Ernest leaped aboard. Then with Anne grasping the reins they went at a rapid clip down the road. "I told Pedro not to tell until the team was missed. And then that I was going to Springertown. That'll put Dad off the track. He'll be wild—but not half as wild as he'll be when he discovers the loss of something else."

Ernest put his arm around her slender waist. "We're off. I don't care where. Oh, Anne, it's too wonderful to be true."

"Well, it's true enough," she replied grimly. "You talk sort of funny for a man who's being hunted for a murder."

"What could you expect? It's turned out you don't hate me—but love me."

"Ernest, you've got to use your haid now, love or no love," she replied seriously. "I'm hoping in the excitement that the cowboys won't think of tracking the buckboard but haid straight for Springertown. But even if they do they cain't catch us. We'll have an all night start."

"Where are we going, Anne?"

"We turn off aboot ten miles beyond Brooks' ranch. It's a fairly good road, but not much used. Shortcut to Snowflake, Showdown, Pine Hill and the New Mexico line. I reckon it'll be pretty safe. No word can reach those towns of your—your fight with Hyslip, before we get there. And once across the line we'll be safe from Dad's outfit."

"Your father has it in for me. I never knew exactly why."

"He never liked you. He was suspicious of you at first. Swore you were no cowboy. Thought you might be snooping. Hyslip he always doted on. Wanted me to marry him. Fancy that—the skylarking dude. And of course Hyslip's cronies will be daid set to catch you. They'd not wait for a sheriff, but lynch you, Ernest. Dad would stand by to see them do it, too."

"Without proof that I killed Hyslip?" queried Ernest.

"Proof—they must have that . . . When are you going to tell me what—how it happened?"

"Not until we are married and safe."

"Maybe you'd better never tell me . . . Say, we'll soon be to Brooks' farm. We want to watch careful heah." She urged the team to a swifter gait, until Ernest saw that they were fairly flying along the road. The night was clear and cold; the stars shone white; the cool wind swept his heated face.

"I'll bet it will be cold later," he said.

"Shore will. There's a heavy robe under the seat. Get it out. You don't have a coat. It'll be mighty cold before morning, I reckon."

Ernest drew it forth and spread it over them. "There's a sack of grain under the seat."

"Good. Do you know, it's strange aboot this. Dad set off for Holbrook, intending to be gone several days and—" Anne broke off, and though Ernest did not know just what she was about to divulge he refrained from questioning her.

They were silent for a while. Ernest kept a sharp watch.

"We passed the lane then. Bars down. Somebody forgot. Brooks never leaves the bars down," he remarked presently.

She slackened the rapid pace of the blacks and kept them to a trot. Ernest felt the need of gloves and coat, for the motion of the buckboard caused the robe to slide down continually. He found his thoughts recurring to the reported killing of Hyslip, growing far more concerned about Nebraskie's welfare than his own. But he was satisfied that Nebraskie surely must have had justification for his act. When the truth was know Hyslip would not be mourned or even defended. Hepford must have some private reason for his championship of the dude cowboy and for implicating Ernest in his killing. Siebert had hinted of that very thing openly in his retort to the rancher. Ernest put that out of his mind for the present. He had all he could do to play his part. He wanted to carry his deception up to the time of his actual marriage with Anne, and if possible, beyond that, clear to the hour when he would be able to confront Hepford and claim ownership of Red Rock Ranch.

That was going to be a thrilling moment when he revealed his true identity to Anne. He tried to picture her surprise when she learned that she had married a wealthy rancher instead of a poor fence-post digger. And perhaps after she recovered from the shock she would not regret too deeply that she was the wife of Ernest Howard Selby. How to avoid discovery when they were being married caused Ernest some concern. It would be difficult, unless he could hurry the ceremony and trust to his bride's excitement to conceal the fact that her husband's name was Selby instead of Howard.

From time to time Anne would turn to peer into his face. He could see dark eyes and the shadowy smile on her pale face. "Don't worry, Ernest. I got you into this and I'll get you out."

"I'm not worrying, I'm too happy to fret—and don't care a darn what happens after." "After we're married. Which will be tomorrow."

She laughed. "So you're more concerned about making me your wife than getting away from my dad's outfit or the sheriff?"

"Reckon I am. If I can have you for my wife one single day I'll cheerfully stand to be hanged."

"Well, I won't. I want you forever . . . Lordy, Ernest, isn't it wonderful that we love each other! If we only had known sooner!"

"I did. I told you. I begged you. Couldn't you guess I was not the kind of man to trifle with?"

"I figured you absolutely wrong. So did everybody else, especially Hyslip."

"You sure did. I'm a bad hombre." replied Ernest cooly. "I'll surprise you yet, too."

"Don't,please. This once is enough for me. I'm punished for all time."

So they talked on, with frequent intervals of silence, and the miles slid past under the buckboard wheels. Presently they turned off the main road, and after that Anne showed great relief. She conserved the strength of the horses, but did not halt them for a rest until long after midnight. It was at the edge of a pine forest, where the road passed under great spreading branches. A brook babbled from somewhere in the darkness and the wind sighed in the tree tops.

"We'd better rest the team and build a fire to warm ourselves," suggested Anne practically.

"Have you any matches?" asked Ernest.

"No. But shore you must have?"

"Nary a match."

"Cain't you build a fire without matches?"

"I'm no wizard."

"Reckon I'll even have to keep you warm, Mr. Tenderfoot."

She drove off the road, into the black shadow of a great pine. Anne insisted that they put the two horse blankets over the horses, and use the rug themselves. So presently Ernest found himself, as one in a dream, under the robe with Anne, his head resting on the sack of grain, and his shoulder serving as a pillow for Anne. In fact she was warm in his arms, almost, and her hair brushed his face.

"This isn't so bad—for runaways," she said softly.

"I think you'd better pinch me to see if I'm awake."

"You'd better sleep some."

"Sleep!"

"Shore. I intend to. It's no time to be sentimental and romantic, Ernest darling. We'll have plenty of time for that after we get you out of the clutches of the lynching party."

Ernest said no more, and lay there marveling, all too conscious of Anne's warm presence. She made only one movement, and that was to take off her gloves. Her left hand nestled at Ernest's neck and her fingers were like ice. A short time afterward, Selby knew from her deep breathing that she had fallen asleep. He saw the stars shining through the dark lacy foliage and he listened to the keening of the wind in the big pines overhead. He wondered what the next day would bring forth, though for his part he never wanted it to dawn. Then hours later the sweet proximity of Anne passed into oblivion.

II

When Ernest awoke the sky was gray and cold. His movement disturbed Anne, who sat up looking wildly about her. But it took her, at most, only an instant to connect the present with the past. She threw back the rug, laughing gaily. "I was shore snug and warm. Roll out, cowboy. You don't seem to be a very ambitious bridegroom."

Ernest rolled out with all the alacrity that his cramped limbs would allow.

"Where's my gloves? . . . . Oh, dear, I lay on my hat . . . . Ernest, we must feed the horses and be on our way even though we'll have to go breakfastless ourselves. There's water heah, but I doubt if the horses will drink."

Ernest set the bag of grain upright. "That was a darn sight harder pillow than you had," he observed.

"Oh, my pillow was fine—that is, after its internal machinery calmed down. Ernest, at first your heart was beating like a trip hammer."

"Humph! Why shouldn't it? Never before did it serve as a pillow for such a beautiful and bewitching head."

"Honest?"

"Yes, honest," he added, shortly.

"Well, I've plenty reason to love you and that's one more. I knew it, though, without your telling me."

"Who's the sentimental one now? What'll we feed the horses with?"

"Nose bags. They must be under the back seat."

It was just daylight when they were finally ready to start. As Anne turned the buckboard back into the road she appeared to discover something on the ground.

"Ernest, we didn't make those tracks," she observed.

Whereupon he discovered both wheel and hoof

tracks in the sandy soil.

"Looks pretty fresh to me," he said.

"They shore were made yesterday. Now who the deuce could be ahaid of us? . . . . Ernest, I don't like that for a cent."

"What do we care so long as they're ahead."

"It might be somebody who'll spread the news."

"That's so. What'll we do?"

"Risk it and go on."

So they did, and the sky reddened in the east, and the sun rose to make the frosty grass sparkle, and the beautiful woodland awoke with life of bird and squirrel. Ernest saw deer, and horses that he was sure must be wild. His enthusiasm did not communicate itself to Anne, who looked serious, and seemed to be shy now that it was broad daylight. She drove for a while, after which Ernest asked to take the reins. And as he was by no means a good driver, he had his hands full with the spirited team. On good stretches of road, however, he did well enough. Once Anne remarked that she might make a Westerner out of him, after all. At length they came to a brook, where the horses drank. Ernest tumbled out and did likewise. But Anne averred she would prefer to remain famished until she could have a cup of coffee and some toast.

They climbed a long gradual slope over a wooded hill, and went on down into more open range country. Selby looked in vain for fences and ranches, but espied neither, and did not see even any signs of cattle until nearly noon. Then they began to descend into lower country, where the rocks and pines vanished, and the cedars of the desert began to manifest themselves. Here cattle dotted the open patches, and at length they came to the first ranch.

"I don't know how far it is yet, but we ought to be coming to Snowflake soon," said Anne anxiously. "I was over this road once years ago."

Her anxiety communicated itself to Ernest, who showed his concern by urging the team forward. The blacks, however, still did not appear to tire.

"How many miles have we come?" he asked once.

"I reckon sixty miles, if not more. This time tomorrow we'll be over the line."

"Anne, we'll be over the matrimonial line today, if I can find a preacher."

She blushed scarlet. "You're shore in a hurry to make me Mrs. Ernest Howard."

"Hurry's no name for it."

"Are you afraid I'll change my mind?"

"You're a bewildering girl, you'll have to admit. I'll take no more chances."

"Ernest, have no fear. You'll never lose me now," she replied wistfully.

From the top of a hill they espied a pretty village down in a valley. Anne said that it was Snowflake. Its green confines covered considerable space, out of which white and gray houses showed, and a church spire, and a large brick edifice.

"Good! I see a church," crowed Ernest, urging the team faster.

"But, darling, there—there is a jail heah, too," faltered Anne.

"Who cares? We can have the preacher come in and marry us there as well as anywhere."

"You beat me all hollow," she returned, puzzled by his careless gaiety, yet at the same time gratified.

So they drove on down into Snowflake, which to Ernest appeared to be a very pretty town, and by no means the little hamlet he had expected it to be.

They entered the town by a long main street, far down which straggled two rows of buildings. The outskirts, however, consisted of small cottages, set well back among trees and gardens. A boy, astride an old gray black-spotted horse, came by.

"Hey, sonny, is there a preacher in this town?" asked Ernest.

"Yes, sir, a new one, just come. Parson Peabody. He lives in thet there house there—where you see the buggy hitched—next to the church."

"Thanks, sonny. Here's a dollar," replied Ernest, gratefully, and he flipped the silver coin to the boy, who dexterously caught it.

"Gee! Much obliged, mister. I bet you're gonna git married."

Ernest was trying to prepare himself for the ordeal ahead. He occupied himself with driving the blacks, and did not look at Anne until they drew up before the house which the boy had pointed out to them. He reined in the team behind the buggy, and was about to step out when Anne clutched his arm.

"Look," she whispered, in sudden agitation.

Ernest looked down the street, naturally expecting to see a posse riding toward them. But the street was vacant and sleepy in the late afternoon sun. Indeed the whole town appeared to be taking a siesta.

"It's Nebraskie and my cousin Dais Brooks," cried Anne.

"Whatever does this mean?"

Ernest wheeled swiftly. Coming down the path from the house were three figures, two of whom were those of his friend and Daisy. Nebraskie was dressed in his best, and it took only another glance to tell that Daisy was also. Ernest sagged on the buckboard seat and stared, thunderstruck.

Then Nebraskie showed sudden excitement. He had discovered the presence of the buckboard and its occupants, and came running up to the gate. He looked paler than Ernest had ever seen him.

"For Gawd's sake, Ernie, is it you?" he demanded.

"I think—it is, Nebraskie—but I'm not sure—of anything anymore," replied Ernest haltingly.

"An' is thet Anne with you?"

"Yes, I guess so. It *was*" replied the Iowan, turning to see that Anne was hiding behind him.

"Did you hear what happened—aboot me?"

"No. I've not heard anything," replied Ernest, studying the cowboy's stern visage.

"What'd you foller us fer, then?"

"Nebraskie, we didn't follow you. We had not the remotest notion you were here," rejoined Ernest, in a voice that permitted no doubt.

"Pard, if I'm not loco I seen thet buckboard an'

team yestiddy as late as four o'clock. An' heah they are in Snowflake."

"That may be, Nebraskie, but it doesn't prove you're not loco."

"Whatinhell—excuse me, Parson," burst out Nebraskie, as Daisy and the third member of the trio joined him. "Ernie, what on earth are *you* doing here?"

"For one thing—Anne and I want to get married," replied Ernest loftily.

"*Whoopee!*" yelled the cowboy. "Thet's what Dais an' I come ter do and we done it! We're married!"

Ernest leaped out of the buckboard and strode the gate. Daisy's strained, pale face, telltale as always, grew rosy. "Congratulations, pard. I'm sure glad . . . . Daisy, I'm going to kiss you. I always wanted to, you know." And Ernest did so quite heartily. "You've got the best fellow in world . . . . Anne, come out of it. Here's your own cousin, with my best friend—and they're married."

"I—I'm not blind," faltered Anne, and she clambered unsteadily out of the buckboard. Her face was pearly white, and her big green eyes were wide with mingled astonishment and pleasure. "Dais, I'm happy for you. I wish you joy," she said, and took the girl in her arms.

"Oh, Anne!" cried Daisy, in a strangled voice, and she clung to her cousin. Ernest's keen senses gathered that there was more agitation here, on the part of both girls, than a mere marriage could account for.

"Hey, come heah, Anne," broke in Nebraskie. "Ernie kissed Dais, an' I'm shore gonna kiss you. Same as he, I always wanted to." And he certainly made good use of his opportunity.

Still the tension did not relax. Ernest felt it, and guessed the reason, though he was sorely perplexed at Nebraskie's advent here in Snowflake. But that could be cleared up in due time. The exigency of the moment called for quick wit and action.

"Parson, will you marry us?" asked Ernest, turning to the mildeyed, pleasant faced little clergyman, who stood by, taking in the scene with amused interest.

"Surely, if the young lady is over eighteen," was the reply. "This is my second day here in Snowflake. And this will be the second wedding ceremony. I consider it propitious."

"You have a marriage certificate?" inquired Ernest hurriedly.

"Assuredly. Come right in," replied the minister. "Your friends can be witnesses."

"Anne, I'll go in and—and fix it with the minister," said Ernest, and he did not try to conceal his excitement. His voice actually thickened and broke. "You come in when I call . . . . Nebraskie, pard, hang on to her. Don't let her run."

"Shore, I'll hang on to her, Ioway," replied the cowboy, and he put a long arm around Anne.

Ernest turned to look at the three smiling people at the gate. Sight of them there was too good to be true. Then he hurried the preacher into the house.

"You are a very impetuous young man," observed the minister smilingly.

"Parson, if you knew the trouble and heartbreak it's taken to win that girl!" burst out Ernest. "But hurry, give me a certificate to fill out . . . . Here's twenty dollars. All I've got with me . . . . Ah! Thank you."

Ernest grasped the paper held out to him, and seating himself at the desk began to fill it out. The minister bent over him. "It's customary for me to do that, young man. But it's all right . . . Miss Anne Hepford, aged twenty . . . . And Ernest Howard Selby—aged twenty-four. Very well. Call the others in."

Ernest went to the door. "Come on, Nebraskie. You and Dais fetch her in."

Nebraskie and the two girls hurried into the front parlor of the parsonage. Ernest, despite his agitation, managed to meet them composedly. Anne was far from pale now. As her eyes met Ernest's he felt a sweet warm rush of emotion.

"Have you a ring ready?" asked the parson, as he took up a Bible, which lay open on the table.

"No," replied Ernest blankly. The blood fled back to his heart. Delay here would be fatal, not only to the marriage, but to the identity he wished to conceal.

Daisy came to the rescue. "Take mine, Ernest . . . . Nebraskie forgot to get one so we used this."

"By gosh, pard, we've gotta buy us some rings when we get to Flaggerstown."

The parson took the ring, and straightaway began to read the service. Ernest was keyed up tightly as he waited, his mouth dry, his veins bursting for the minister to begin. Presently came the query: "Do you Ernest, take this woman—"

"Yes!" he burst out loudly, and to his joy the minister passed over the interruption, and went on. The end came swiftly. Anne held out a trembling hand to receive the ring on her finger, and her "Yes" came sweetly and demurely from her heart. It was over. She was his wife. The room seemed to whirl about him. He embraced Anne in a rush of love and gratitude, careless of the onlookers.

"Oh, it's too good to be true!" he exclaimed softly. "Here, Anne, sit down and sign your name . . . . Hurry, dearest . . . . There! Sign there!" He hung over her, and she wrote her name without a glance at the contents of the document. Then Ernest lifted her up and took the paper from her hands, and as one beside himself, while the others smiled, he dashed his own name down and handed the certificate to the minister. In another moment the ceremony was ended without a hitch. Ernest folded the precious paper and waved it at Anne.

"You're my wife. Here's my proof. And I'm the happiest man in the world."

"Yes—I—I'm happy, too, but Ernest, we must go—you know. We must hurry."

"Surely," replied Ernest, as he buttoned his vest over the marriage certificate that now reposed safely in his pocket. "But we must have something to eat first. I'm starved. I didn't feel it before, but I do now."

"Same heah," corroborated Nebraskie. "What's the hurry? We're all married now an' nothin' cain happen. There's a hotel heah. Let's eat."

Anne still seemed to be a bit dazed. Between them they led her outdoors. The preacher followed as far as the gate, pleased with the happiness he had bestowed, and there he bade them good-by. Once seated again in the buckboard Anne begged: "Ernest, let's not stop heah. We must hurry."

"But child, there's no risk. No one save Nebraskie and Daisy know we're here."

"Any minute someone might come."

"Sure. Only the chance is slim. We can't go without eating forever."

So he prevailed upon her, and they drove to the hotel. While the girls went upstairs Ernest and Nebraskie took the horses round to the barn.

"Might as wall unhitch, pard," said Nebraskie. "We'll spend the night heah."

"Suits me," replied Ernest shortly.

"Say, you're shore loco," went on Nebraskie, his keen gray eyes on his friend. "What's eatin' you?"

"A lot," replied Ernest.

"You heahed aboot me?"

"Not a damn word. I told you," flashed Ernest.

"Wal, you needn't jump down my throat. Doggone it, I reckon I done you a good turn."

They saw to the needs of the horses; and then Nebraskie dragged Ernest into a stall, and after peering around to make sure they were alone, he whispered: "Now spill it, you blankfaced idjit!"

Ernest drew a long breath. "Yesterday

afternoon—or when was it?—I saw Hepford and Hyslip drive by Brooks' place. And I jumped at my chance to—to go down to Red Rock. I went. Waited till dark. Then I slipped down to the house. I—I busted into Anne's room—"

"Whatinhell fer? My Gawd, Ernie, I'm worried aboot you," interrupted Nebraskie, red in the face.

"Shut up. This is my turn to talk," went on Ernest. "I busted into Anne's room. She was in bed. She'd been reading. She was scared stiff . . . . Well, that was what I wanted. I was aiming to scare her, among other things. We were having it hot and heavy—she sure I had come to kill her—or worse—because she had treated me so rotten—when Hepford knocked on the door. It was good I locked it. He wanted to come in, but she wouldn't let him. Then he said there had been hell to pay—in substance that I had killed Hyslip—that they were going to lynch me. He went away—and then—well, Nebraskie, I just can't tell you what did happen. But it turned out that Anne really loved me and swore she would run off with me—get me across the state border. I never told her that I didn't kill Hyslip. I knew you did and I was sure sick about it. But I let her believe I had because I wanted to see how she'd take it . . . . She was great, Nebraskie. She helped me outside, met me down in the lane, she stole the buckboard, she drove all night—and here we are."

Nebraskie gripped Ernest with stiff fingers. His eyes shone like fire.

"Didn't I tell you she was game? Thet she'd

come out true? But, Gawd Almighty man! You cain't let her think thet you're a murderer any longer. Fer I killed Hyslip an' it was a job I'm sure proud of."

"For Lord's sake, tell me!" cried Ernest passionately.

"I came back to the ranch aboot four o'clock," began Nebraskie, cool and easy. "Sam an' Hawk was with me, but they put the hosses away while I went to the house. I heahed Dais cry out. An' I heahed a tusslin'. The door was shet. I peeped in the winder, an' there was Dude Hyslip with Dais in his arms. I looked long enough to make shore Dais was fightin' him. An' pard, thank Gawd she was— like a little wildcat! Hyslip always had Dais locoed, but when it come to the pinch she was game . . . . Wal, I was lookin' around fer somethin to bust in the door when Sam an' Hawk arrived. "What's up?'they says. An' I said, 'Bust open thet door damn quick!' When the two flopped agin it—smash! It gave in. Sam lodged agin the doorpost, but Hawk fell in. An' thet crazy fool shot him. I had just enough sense left not to face the open door. So I ran to the winder. I shot Hyslip through the glass, but hit him low down. He came out a yellin. An' he shot at Sam jest as I bored him agin. Funny how nervous I was, pard. It turned out afterward thet either of them shots would hev done fer him, in time. But Hyslip was shore wavin' his gun on me when I killed him."

"Good Lord!" ejaculated Ernest, in mingled relief and horror. "But don't say he killed Hawk?"

"Nope, Hawk got it through the shoulder an' a

madder man I never seen. Dais was in a faint. Wal, we fixed Hawk up temperary. Meanwhile Dais come round of her own accord. Brooks hitched up the wagon an' packed Hawk off to Holbrook, tellin us to foller. After Dais an' I'd thought it over we decided to come over heah an' git married, so's to have thet done when we got to town .... We left Hyslip lyin' where he fell .... I reckon now thet heah's whut happened. Hyslip an' Hepford split up fer some reason. Hyslip went back to Brooks' house, an' findin' Dais alone he lost his haid agin. Then Hepford must hev come back later, an' he jest put the blame on you. Or mebbe Magill an' Davis or Pollard did thet little job. An I reckon thet's aboot all."

"It's bad enough, but thank Heaven you can't be held .... Nebraskie, you're going on to Holbrook, then?"

"Shore. It'll save some investigatin'."

"Hepford put a posse after me, sure as you're born. Suppose they happen along here?"

"Wal, I'd stop them darn pronto. Reckon, though, thet ain't likely. Let's go in an' tell Anne the truth."

"Perhaps Daisy has already."

"No siree. I told Dais to keep mum."

Upon returning to the hotel Ernest and his friend found their wives in their separate rooms. Anne had her hat and coat on and seemed nervously anxious to leave Snowflake without delay.

"Well, let's see Nebraskie and Daisy first. Then if you still want to hurry away, we'll start pronto," replied her husband.

"Ernest, how you talk! I'm sure Daisy knows. She acted so strange. She couldn't keep the tears out of her eyes."

Ernest crossed the hall with Anne and led her into the presence of Daisy and Nebraskie. It was a large light room. Nebraskie looked cool and relaxed, Daisy nervously solicitous.

Anne opened the conversation. "Daisy, you and your husband are on a honeymoon.... But Ernest and I—are fleeing for his life. As he won't tell you I must. He—"

"Now Anne, just wait a little," interposed Nebraskie, in his drawling voice. "Shore there's a mistake around heah somewheres. There cain't be any need of you two fleein'. Cause—"

"But Nebraskie, my dad has set his men on Ernest's trail," cried Anne, her eyes desperate and dark with anxiety. "They hate Ernest. They'll hang him."

"Aw, thet's a bit exaggerated, Anne. What on earth fer?"

"Ernest killed Hyslip. It was my fault. Oh, I was rotten to Ernest. I know he's innocent of murder. He shot Hyslip in self-defense. But *they* won't believe that. They won't give my—my husband a chance. We won't be safe until we're across the line."

"Anne, darling, wait. Let us say a word. You haven't considered that maybe—perhaps your father—made a mistake," interrupted Ernest.

"Mistake? What aboot?" returned Anne, nonplussed. She gazed from one to the other. And when Daisy began to cry she turned to comfort her.

"Why shore—aboot this heah killin' of Hyslip," said Nebraskie, feeling his way. "My pard Ernie, now, he couldn't hev done it, Anne. He jest couldn't."

"Why not?" she implored weakly, a terrible hope in her eyes.

"Wal, in the first place Ernie wasn't around when it happened. I was the one who killed him."

Anne gave a gasp, and reeling, would have fallen if Nebraskie had not caught her in his arms.

III

Stricken with remorse, Ernest took his wife's unconscious form out of Nebraskie's arms and laid her on the bed. Daisy removed her hat, and the two of them managed to get her coat off, after which they bathed her white face with cold water. At length her eyelids flickered, then opened, to reveal two tragic wells of consciousness.

"There! She's come to," whispered Daisy.

"Aw, I'm shore glad. She looked daid. Think of Anne Hepford keelin' over like thet."

"Anne, darling—you fainted," said Ernest, greatly relieved, as he held her hands.

Nebraskie drew Daisy away. "Say, folks, we'll go have a special dinner fixed up." And he left Daisy in a haste that gave evidence of great concern.

"All right, but not too soon," called the Iowan after them, and then closed the door. When he returned to the bed it was to discover a new Anne

Hepford.

"Ernest, is it true?" she faltered.

"Is what true, honey?"

"That you didn't—kill Hyslip?"

"Certainly is true, I'm happy to confess. But, darling, I never *said* I did."

"You didn't deny it."

"No, I let you think so."

"Oh, why did you deceive me?" she asked, reproachfully.

Ernest leaned over, holding her hands, and gazing deep into the eyes that at last expressed her true soul.

"Well, you took it for granted. You were so shocked, you blamed yourself so passionately that I just couldn't bear to tell you," explained Ernest.

"Ernest, you are pretty wonderful, too. I don't know just how—but you are," she replied dreamily, and she slipped a hand free to touch his cheek tenderly. "You were cruel. You've no idea of the torture I endured."

"I endured some myself, little wife," he said, significantly.

"I'd forgotten. I am your wife . . . . Oh, thank God you didn't kill that cowboy. Ernest, I'm no chickenhearted girl. I'm western. I'm not afraid of death—or of a man who takes a life in a just cause. But the fact that I thought I was to blame is what crucified me."

"I might have done it. I packed a gun for that very reason."

"But you didn't . . . . Let me up, dear . . . . I feel giddy."

Ernest led her to a big chair, and sitting down he

drew Anne into his lap. It was not many moments before the natural ruddy color had been restored to her cheeks.

"They might come back," she whispered, protesting.

"Who cares? Anne, I can't get used to the idea you love me and that I've the right to embrace you and kiss you whenever I like," he rejoined.

"If I remember correctly you did something of—of that sort before you had any right at all.... Oh, I tried to fight against you. To my shame I confess it—after that first time I—I was crazy for your kisses."

"Glory be! And you never let me guess it!" cried Ernest ruefully.

"You acted as if you did.... Ernest, please tell me where, why and how Nebraskie killed Hyslip?"

Ernest took rather a long time for his recital of Nebraskie's story.

"Served him right!" she flashed, with green fire in her eyes. "Ernest, I was always afraid of him. When I rode with him I was careful never to get off my horse. I rode, and that's all, believe me.... I'm sorry for Daisy. Poor kid! She shore was hypnotized by that cowboy.... It might have been worse. I think Nebraskie is a noble fellow. He must love her dearly. It will come out all right in the end."

"I hope so.... And that our love and marriage does the same."

"We shore have a lot to think of," she said, with an arm around his neck. "Reckon I ought to be scared still of what's ahaid of us. But I'm not. I can work. You'd never believe it, Ernest, but I can cook, bake, wash, sew. Honest, I can. Reckon I was born to be a cowboy's wife. We'll pioneer it somewhere. I can chop wood, too, and I believe I could handle a plow."

"I hope you don't have to be a drudge for me. Maybe we'll find a way. Don't you think you could make a rancher out of me?"

"I sure could. Only," she sighed, "it can't be Red Rock now! When I think of how I loved Red Rock—that always it seemed mine—I feel sort of sick. Imagine, Ernest. When the news first came that the new owner of Red Rock was coming out to take charge—I—made up my mind to marry him! Young or old, I meant to. That shows you how I love that ranch. And now—"

"My, what a calculating creature you were! And I'll bet you'd have done it too. No man could resist you, Anne. But you married me, a poor cowboy instead," he ended exultantly.

"So it appears. I'm not sorry, Ernest. I'll never have any regrets. It'll be the making of me."

"It'll have to be the making of us both. But Anne, let's postpone talking about all them serious things for the present. At least until—"

"How can we, you goose? Our problems begin now. I feel so free, so happy at the release from that terror for you—why, I can face anything."

"Even life with a poverty stricken, would-be cowboy?" he asked smilingly.

"Yes, as long as that poverty stricken, would-be cowboy is you," she nodded gravely, smoothing his hair.

"You make me feel very humble—and very

proud, my dear," said her husband in a voice that was little above a whisper.

"Ah—I—I reckon it doesn't make any difference now," whispered Anne, surrendering to his embrace.

The simplicity of Anne's statement brought Ernest sharply to his senses.

"Anne, I—I must tell you something—we can't be really husband and wife truly—until—"

"What do you mean?" she queried, aghast, while the red mantled from neck to temples.

"Simply this. I won't—I can't take advantage of your love and your becoming my wife—all that it implies—until I can do so honestly. It's a horrible temptation to continue as we are. But—"

"Ernest!" she cried, clasping him wildly.

"Anne, I've deceived you—basely."

"Aboot Hyslip? But I know now."

"Not that. Something very much worse. I hope you'll still love me, but you might not."

"Oh, what is it?"

"I can't tell you yet."

"Ernest, it's not—you have someone else?"

"No, not that."

"You never loved any other girl?"

"Honestly, I never did."

"There's no reason why I cain't be your wife?"

"No, indeed."

"Then what in the world have you done?"

"I won't tell you now."

"When?"

"In a few days. After we go to Holbrook and disprove the charge your father laid upon me. And have it out with him."

"Pooh! You're afraid of Dad?" she exclaimed, in sudden relief.

"Yes, I am a little. He'll be a bad customer. He never liked me. And Hyslip and his cronies hated me. Naturally that set Hepford even more against me. Then the day we came back from our ride—I was mighty upset. I was determined to find out something to his discredit. Siebert's talk told me a lot."

"Shore, it told me a lot, too," rejoined Anne bitterly. "It justified my fears. If I'd had any sense I'd have realized Dad was being dishonest. I knew in my heart, when he drew all that cash out of the bank, and told me we'd leave Red Rock presently—I knew he was dishonest. Siebert knew it, too."

"Well, dear, I know it, also," returned Ernest. "He had discharged me. You had flouted me. I determined to get proof of my suspicions. It was partly for that reason that I broke into your house. . . . Anne, I stole the little blue book you wouldn't let me look into. I stole it that night. Here it is in my pocket now."

"So that was it," she murmured.

"Yes. Hepford drove up to the porch. Almost surprised me in his office. I couldn't get by, so I ran down the hall. That was how I happened to come into your bedroom. Oh, what a lucky thing for me. But if you'd only known it—my heart was in my throat."

"Then, it was not to—to revenge yourself on me that you came?"

"Indeed it was not."

"How things come aboot! But I'm glad—

Ernest—*glad* . . . . When you burst in there—white as a sheet—with eyes like black blades, I just wilted. I thought you'd come to—well—to do something after Hyslip's style. And now that I'm your wife I can confess . . . . No! I won't confess that. Someday, maybe."

"Anne, I think I can guess. And talk about your savages! But I loved you too deeply for revenge—or anything like that. No, I went to the ranch house to steal this little book."

As he took it out of his pocket a thick envelope came with it. "What's this? Oh, your letter, I must read it. But I no longer need it to prove to me that you are true blue. I'll never need any proof of that anymore, darling."

"Read it, Ernest, but not now. First let's see what's in Dad's book."

"No. It might make you unhappy," returned Ernest, replacing both letter and book in his pocket. "That can wait."

"Ernest, I'm a thief too," confessed Anne boldly.

"How so?"

"Dad entrusted me that wallet of money he drew from the bank last time he was in town. When he leaves the house he always does that—well, we had to have money. So I fetched it with me."

"Anne, you stole for me!"

"I shore did. It hurts now that you're not a fugitive from the law. I reckon I'll have to return it to Dad—even though I feel I ought to keep it for the new owner of Red Rock, when he comes. He'd probably reward me, Ernest. And you and I must have enough money to get away with. We cain't stay heah."

"I'm not sure what we can do. Where's that wallet, Anne?"

"In my bag."

"I'll get it," decided Ernest with alacrity, and disengaging himself from Anne he left the room to cross the hall into their room. His fingers were not steady as he opened Anne's bag. What a complication of events. He found a large leather wallet, so full that it appeared about to burst. Ernest could not resist opening it far enough to see if the contents really were money. His eyes popped. Closing the wallet he raced with it back to Anne, scarcely thinking to conceal his exultancy.

"I declare, Anne, this is great," he said, waving the wallet.

"Ernest, are you going to give in to temptation?" she queried, with grave concern. "Even if Dad has been dishonest that's no reason for us to be. Because I stole the money. And if you make me keep it you'll be dishonest too."

"What'll we do, darling?" he asked, boldly, realizing that here was the supreme test of Anne Hepford. "I gave my last dollar to marry you. We'll have a long hard fight before we can have a home and all the things you're accustomed to."

"Ernest. You frighten me . . . . I'd have been glad to spend it—every dollar—to save your life—or a long term in jail. But you're free. We're both young, strong, and we've got brains. We won't steal, Ernest. But we might fairly put that money away—in the bank—for its rightful owner."

Ernest shouted out loud in his gladness, and his antics opened Anne's eyes wide. "Are you plain loco, boy?"

"I'm just so glad I'll—I'll burst. You can't understand how I feel. But that you'd steal to save me and won't steal to make us rich—what can I say! You're wonderful."

"Am I? Love is blind, Ernest . . . . Put that wallet away before Nebraskie and Daisy come back."

Ernest had difficulty in stuffing it into his inside coat pocket, and then it bulged noticeably. "Lordy, I can't wait to count it."

"I did," laughed Anne.

"How much is here?"

"Guess."

"Several thousand, I'm sure."

"Do you think a big rancher makes so much over as little money as that? Ernest, there's over forty thousand dollars in that wallet."

Ernest sat down suddenly, his eyes popping.

"No!"

"Shore is. We'll count it again when we're alone. I don't know if it's a good idea though. You might . . . ."

A knock on the door interrupted them.

"That you, Nebraskie? Come in,' shouted Ernest gaily.

The door opened to admit the lanky cowboy and Daisy. They were all eyes.

"Well Anne, you come to fine, I'm glad to see. An' say, pard, what's eatin' you?"

"Starvation. Is the dinner near ready?"

"You bet. An' it's gonna be a humdinger. Come on. Let's forget our troubles."

Notwithstanding Nebraskie's enthusiasm, and a bountiful spread by the landlady, the dinner was not a marked success. Ernest, despite his assertion that he was starved, had to force himself to eat. And the girls were evidently too excited to be hungry. Conversation lagged.

"Wal," drawled Nebraskie, "you gurls shore hev long faces an' dewy eyes. What's the matter? There ain't nuthin' wrong. If what people say is true—that the consummashun of women's happiness is gettin married, you both ought to be turrible full of joy."

"I am, Nebraskie," declared Anne, smiling through her tears. "But it's a little too soon—right now."

"Don't be a fool," retorted Daisy, giving her husband a disapproving look. "How can we be gay?"

"Ioway, let's you an' me celebrate," said the cowboy, turning to Ernest. "Mebbe if we got ourselves good an' drunk our wifes would lose their glum faces, anyhow."

"It's no laughing matter, Nebraskie," declared Ernest. "You're only bluffing. Deep down in your gizzard you've got bridegroom jitters yourself."

At the conclusion of the dinner, Ernest suggested that they go on toward Holbrook. There were still several hours of daylight. They could drive until late and stop at some ranch house; then get into town by noon next day.

"Wha-at?" demanded Nebraskie. "Sleep in some stall or haymow on the first night of our honeymoon—when we could stay at this heah nice quiet hotel?"

"Be reasonable, pard. To be sure it's our honeymoon, but you'll allow, no ordinary one," protested Ernest.

"Ioway, I been dreamin' an' prayin fer this ever since I laid eyes on Dais," protested the cowboy, in his turn.

"Nebraskie, I've entertained something of the same hope ever since I saw Anne," went on Ernest, with a laugh at the evident embarrassment of the two brides. "Listen now, you Romeo. There are some things to settle up before we start on this honeymoon."

"What, fer instance?"

"Well, this late escapade of yours—ridding Red Rock of a very undesirable individual. And looking out for new jobs to come back to—after our honeymoon. Let's go on to Holbrook, then back to Red Rock, and then, after all is fixed up fine, have our honeymoon."

"The four of us?" asked Daisy eagerly, her dark eyes shining. "Oh, I'd love that."

"It does sound nice. I—I believe I approve," added Anne, who evidently wanted to help Ernest, but was not completely sure he was not out of his mind.

Nebraskie stared hard at his friend.

"We might even raise money enough to go to California," went on Ernest, trying to be casual.

"Wal, pard, now I savvy what turned Anne's

haid. It's your silver tongue," burst out Nebraskie, in admiration mixed with wistfulness. "My Gawd, I wisht we could. But I'm near broke. An you air broke. Dais hasn't any money. Have you, Anne?"

"I reckon Ernest can raise some. But wouldn't he be crazy to spend it on honeymooning, when there's no more in sight?"

"Shore we'd be crazy," admitted the cowboy. "But I'd like to go thet crazy once . . . . As fer a job, Ioway, I'm goin' to work with Dais's father. It'll be slow buildin' up a payin' ranch, but I see somethin' shore ahead, anyway."

"Cowboy, the way to make money out of Brooks' place is to irrigate, put most of the land in alfalfa, and run your cattle out on the range." said Ernest, most businesslike.

"I'm a sun of a gun," ejaculated Nebraskie. "Never thought of thet. Neither did Sam. Ioway, you're not such a dunce at thet. It's a darn good idee."

Anne was so pleased with Ernest's sound ideas that her face grew tender.

"It is indeed," she said. "That is precisely what Dad meant to do with the farm, when he'd driven Brooks off."

"Oh, I'll be a rancher someday," said Ernest, laconically. "How could I help it, with such a wife? . . . . Well, Nebraskie, shall we forego our honeymoon, and get to moving toward town?"

"Shore. I reckon I'm gonna stick to you like a plaster, from now on." rejoined Nebraskie.

While the two were hitching up Nebraskie observed thoughtfully: "Ioway, you're the damnedest, originalest, mysteriest, best pard I ever had."

Soon they were driving north on another road. They passed several ranches before dark, but after night fell they did not come to another until it was so late that Nebraskie advised not awakening the owner. They drove on to a cedar woods, where they built a fire, unhitched the horses, and made camp under a clump of cedars. They managed to keep warm, at least. Dawn came presently, and soon afterward they were travelling swiftly on the last lap of their journey. Before noon they were in Holbrook.

IV

When Ernest thought what he was going to do, now that he had arrived at Holbrook, he found himself at a loss. As he drove the buckboard up the main street he espied Nebraskie's rig halting in front of the hotel, where several other vehicles stood. Two or three men strode across the pavement to meet Nebraskie. One of them he recognized to be Brooks.

When Ernest hauled up beside them the rancher's broad face was wreathed in smiles. A quick glance at Nebraskie and Daisy satisfied Ernest that all was well.

"Wal, an' what air you doin' heah?" queried Brooks in surprise.

"I've been getting married, Sam," replied Ernest happily. "Nebraskie hasn't got a corner on all the girls."

"Fer the land's sake!" exploded the rancher, throwing up his hands. "You ain't gone and married Anne Hepford?"

"I should think one look at her would be sufficient to convince you," replied the Iowan blandly.

It would have been, but Brooks took more than one. "Wal, I'll be doggoned.... Howard, you're a lucky cuss. As for you Anne, wal, I reckon, if looks count much you're as happy as you air lucky. Bless you both."

"Tell me pronto. How's Hawk?" interrupted Ernest.

"He's all right. Little lame in his shoulder, but nothin' serious for such a tough customer like him. I'm pickin' him up at Babbitt's. We're drivin' off right away. Jest almost missed you."

"Then—there's no—no trouble ahead for Nebraskie?"

"Nope. None in the least. Siebert an' me fixed thet. The sheriff drove out this mawin' fer Red Rock. We're to meet him there."

"Well," ejaculated Ernest with a deep sigh of relief.

Brooks turned to Nebraskie: "I reckon, son, you'd better go along with us."

"Shore, Sam. We'll hev somethin' to eat, an' ketch up with you."

"I'll stop at Miller's."

Ernest leaped at a solution to his problem. "Anne, you go along with Daisy and Nebraskie.

I'll follow as quickly as—"

"See heah," exploded Nebraskie. "Ain't we gonna ever hev any honeymoon at all?"

"Leave that to me," retorted the Iowan, laughing.

"Wal, all right, if you'll promise thet after the fuss an' funeral are over we'll go off somewhere an' be happy fer a coupla days anyhow."

"I promise, Nebraskie."

"Darling, for a brand new married man, you seem rather anxious to get rid of your wife," interposed Anne, her large eyes studying him quizzically.

"It does look a little that way," rejoined Ernest, laughing. "But, dearest, I imagine your father will not take our marriage as calmly as Daisy's father did hers. Wouldn't it be better for you to see him first?"

"Yes, it shore would," replied Anne, a little grimly. "But you forget. What'll I say aboot the money?"

"Oh!" Ernest certainly had to think hard. "Anne, you must pretend surprise at its absence. Then—when I come down I'll explain."

Anne gazed at him dubiously, but his frankness disarmed her for the moment.

"Very well. I—I reckon you're right," she conceded thoughtfully. "I don't want to stay heah an hour longer than necessary, with that storm hanging over my haid."

Ernest leaped out to help her down. She whispered, her hand on his: "If you didn't come back it'd—kill me."

"Anne!"

She said no more but when she got up between Daisy and Nebraskie she gave him a long look that he would remember as long as he lived.

"Ioway, when'll you come?" queried Nebraskie. "We ain't gonna start our honeymoon till you do. Shore if we did it'd plumb kill Anne. I heahed her say so."

"Well, let's go if we're going," cried Anne sharply, and Daisy pummeled Nebraskie with a vigorous little fist. Reluctantly, the cowboy took up the reins and clucked to the horses.

"Wal, I'm so glad over thet I could bust," declared Brooks, fervently, as he watched them drive down the street. Anne looked back once more before the buggy disappeared down the road.

"So long, Sam. I've got some things to do," said the Iowan quietly. "I'll see you at home, maybe tomorrow or next day surely."

Ernest first called upon his lawyer, Jefford Smith, who was greatly pleased to see him.

"I was trying to make up my mind to go down to Red Rock," said Smith, after greeting him. "You are delaying too long. Hepford is planning on shipping cattle to New Mexico. He has acquired a ranch there."

"Well, a lot has happened to prevent me. One thing of which was I fell in love with Hepford's daughter."

"No!"

"And I married her, too," declared Ernest.

The lawyer was thunderstruck. "Good heavens, young man! Unless you mean to let Hepford get away with wholesale robbery, you've surely complicated the case."

"Mr. Smith, I won't let him get away with any more property. But of course I won't put him in jail or even disgrace him. That, of course, is for his daughter's sake."

"You're a very magnanimous man. Excuse me, but is she deserving of such a sacrifice?" returned the lawyer bluntly.

"She's worth more."

"Hepford has robbed you of approximately two hundred thousand dollars."

"Sure that hurts. But I've got nearly forty thousand of it back. At least I have the money. The disposition of it depends on your judgment."

"How on earth did you get such a sum from him?" demanded the astonished attorney.

"Well, he entrusted it to Anne, his daughter, and I took it."

"Good, put it in the bank at once."

"I will sir . . . . And I have something else. I stole a little blue book, a private ledger in which Hepford kept his personal accounts. Can you recall the statements in my uncle's papers, which I showed you?"

"Yes, enough to make comparisons. Let me see this ledger."

It did not take the keen lawyer long to digest the contents of the little book. Closing it, he said, "You have him pat. Now what are your instructions?"

"How soon can I leave for Red Rock?"

"Right away."

"I must rest the horses. Say tomorrow morning early."

"The earlier the better."

"Daylight then, at the hotel . . . . Oh, yes, there's one more thing. I need some money."

"I can lend you any reasonable sum. But why not draw on that you have? It's yours. There will never be any court proceedings."

"Gosh!" ejaculated Ernest, and rushed away.

On his way to the bank he happened to think that to deposit such a sum of money as he had in his possession might well rouse suspicion on the part of the bank officials. There was only one bank in town. Hepford had drawn the identical sum there not very long before. Ernest decided he would risk less by carrying it on his person.

His first errand was to the jeweler's. And this was an occasion. Not for nothing had he looked so long at Anne's fingers, nor studied the ring Daisy had loaned her to be married with. He purchased a gold wedding ring, and then a solitaire ring, the stone in which was a very beautiful blue-white diamond, the finest the jeweler had in stock. Then, such was Ernest's exultation, he bought another solitare that he would tender to Nebraskie to give Daisy. He felt hugely delighted with himself.

From the jeweler's he repaired to the emporium where he had once obtained chaps, gloves, spurs and sombrero. He was remembered.

"Want something rich in cowboy togs," he said. "No flash or phony stuff."

There appeared to be a vast assortment of things for riders of the range. What an extravagant class cowboys were. Ernest bought boots with high tops of decorated kangaroo leather, as soft as kid; silver mounted Mexican spurs; fringed buckskin and scarf; and lastly a black leather gun belt and holster containing a white bone-handled gun.

"Some Texas Jack died heah sudden with his boots on, an' I got these," explained the merchant. "Second hand, yes, but all the better for a little wear."

Ernest carried his purchases to his hotel room, thinking the while how his new regalia would make Anne gasp and those Red Rock cowboys stare and gape. His mental state was such that he could scarcely eat and he almost forgot to order the buckboard fetched round at dawn. It seemed no time at all when he was awakened by a thumping on his door. Through the window he could see that another day was dawning—a day that perhaps was to be a very important one in his life.

Hepford's black team was noted for its swift trips to town and back. By three o'clock in the afternoon Ernest halted where Brooks' lane branched off the Red Rock road.

"Now, Mr. Smith," said Ernest, "You drive on to the ranch. Leave the horses at the barn and go hunt up Hepford. Tell him simply this—that the new owner of Red Rock will be there pronto, you are his lawyer, and you want to know what he's going to do about an accounting. I'll get my papers and follow you immediately."

"I like the job . . . . But, does your wife know *you* are young Selby?"

"She does not. Don't you tell her or anybody."

"Very good. I'll expect you shortly after I arrive," returned the lawyer, and then he drove on.

Ernest strode rapidly down the lane, absorbed in thought. He had planned exactly what to do and say, how he was going to act, up to a certain point. That point was when he finally found himself alone with Anne. As he thought of that moment his heart came up in his throat. When he stooped to slide between the bars of Brooks' gate his ear was assailed by a stentorian: "Whoopee!"

Nebraskie was standing in the open door. "Folks, come heah," he called to those within. "It's Ioway. Look at him!"

"Howdy, boy," drawled Siebert, with his hawk eyes twinkling.

"How're you, boss?" flashed Ernest, his quick eyes noting no change in the foreman, except a slight pallor.

"Me? Aw, I'm plumb fine."

"Brooks, how'd it all come out? About the sheriff?"

"They was heah yestiddy," replied the rancher cheerily. "Looked around some, at these bullet holes in the doorpost. Then they packed Hyslip off to Springer. I made shore they'd stop at Hepford's to tell him the news."

"Will you hitch up your two seater and take us all down to Red Rock?" asked Ernest eagerly.

"Shore I'll hitch up, but what fer do you want us to go—me in particular?"

"Sam, the boy figgers he may need his friends," put in Siebert persuasively.

"Wal, then, shore I'll go," replied the rancher, and he moved away toward the barn.

Nebraskie walked round and round Ernest, gazing with experienced eyes, as he inspected the Iowan's new outfit.

"You locoed son-of-a-gun from Ioway! .... Silver spurs an' Mex at thet! Kangaroo tops. An' them velvet pants! .... Peep at thet gun, Hawk. Look at it! .... Ernie, I'm shore knocked flat to think you'd go in debt like this."

"Come here, you long lean cowpuncher," retorted Ernest, dragging him aside. "Look! Is this what you wanted?" And Ernest produced the diamond solitaire. The cowboy's eyes popped, his jaw dropped, for only a moment, when his back was toward the others.

"Dais, come heah," he drawled, his old cool easy self again. "Looka heah .... Gimme your hand. I ast Ioway to fetch this to you .... Doggone! It's perfect."

After one little joyous scream Daisy became petrified. Ernest left them to their amazed rapture. He did not want to betray then the emotion that gripped him. But Nebraskie soon caught him, swung a long arm around his shoulders.

"Pard, did ya rob the bank?"

"No," laughed Ernest.

"Hold up anybody?"

"Well, not quite."

"Went in debt fer us! My Gawd, pard I reckon ya got the same fer Anne."

"Sure did. Look again, pard."

Nebraskie gazed mutely. At last he burst out: "Jumpin' broncos! We're ruined. It'll take all over lives to pay them debts. But I'm game: I'd a done it myself."

Not until the two-seated wagon had reached the Red Rock corrals and barns did Selby again acquire the cool self-control that he had determined to show now that the big moment had come. The time had arrived for the big showdown, when Red Rock was to become his own.

They reached the long bunkhouse, upon the porch of which lounged the cowboys Lunky Pollard, Steve Monell, Bones Magill and Shep Davis. They were staring at the arrival of Brooks' two-seater with wide-open eyes.

"Sam, I'll get off heah an' pack my duds, roll my bed an' get my saddle," said Nebraskie.

"Hadn't Hawk better get down too?" queried Brooks in a low tone.

"Reckon I had, Nebraskie," replied the foreman.

"What fer?" asked the cowboy mildly.

"Wal, Shep, anyhow, is a bad hombre. He looks ugly."

"You go with my husband," said Daisy peremptorily to Siebert.

"Wal, reckon all the rest of my life now I gotta be chaparooned," complained Nebraskie. "But if you want to know it, those boys won't kick up nothin.' They'd been all right but fer Hyslip."

"You're talkin' sense there, Nebraskie."

They got out and slowly walked toward the bunkhouse. Ernest watched them long enough to assure himself there was no need for concern, then he braced himself for the ordeal at hand. Brooks reined in his team before the big ranch house, that had never before seemed so impressive to its new owner.

"You follow me," said Ernest, to father and

daughter, and leaped out of the wagon to go quickly up the steps.

The office door was open. Ernest looked in to see the room was vacant. He heard voices in the living room. Entering he espied Anne standing beside the open fireplace. She looked grave. Mr. Smith sat opposite, and Hepford, white and shaken, halted in his pacing the floor before the porch windows.

"Get out of heah!" he almost shouted. "You cain't pull the wool over my eyes as you did over Anne's. She's confessed she's your wife. It wasn't necessary for you to come. Get out of heah, an' take her with you. I've business with this lawyer. We're expectin' the new owner of Red Rock."

"Mr. Hepford, he has come," interposed Smith, rising.

"What?" snapped Hepford.

"Young Selby has arrived," returned the lawyer, indicating Ernest. "This young man you once employed as a cowboy is Ernest Howard Selby."

"*Wha-aat!*" shouted Hepford, with a roar that was like a thunderclap, and indeed his face resembled a thundercloud.

"Yes, Mr. Hepford, I am Ernest Selby," spoke up Ernest composedly, and he stepped forward to hand the small valise that contained his papers to the lawyer.

Hepford suddenly turned white and flopped into a chair, a beaten man. Ernest took a fleeting glance at Anne. That one glance was enough. Another would have unnerved him completely. As he turned again to face the two men he saw her, out of the corner of his eye, walk with bowed head out of the room. How he had to fight to keep from rushing to her.

"Mr. Hepford," said Smith, in a professional tone, "you will go over these papers with me."

"To hell—with papers!" muttered the rancher thickly. "If this Iowa tenderfoot is Selby's nephew—why thet's enough for me. I quit. I'll get out at once, this very night."

"Very good, but there are some other matters we have to wind up first. I was just suggesting before Selby's arrival—" went on Smith.

"Let's make it short and sweet," interrupted Selby, and at that moment he was glad to see Hawk Siebert come in quietly. "Mr. Hepford, I've had the great good fortune to win the hand of your daughter. Naturally I have no intention of ruining you or of making her unhappy. We need not even go over your irregularities, such as I have proof of in a little blue ledger I appropriated from your desk . . . I have, also, the forty thousand dollars you entrusted to Anne. She believed I had killed Hyslip and took the money so that we could get out of the country. If you withdraw claim to that, and this ranch, and all your other Arizona interests in the bank and otherwise, I will exact no more. There will be no publicity whatever."

"Howard, I—I'll do thet," responded Hepford thickly, staring with astonishment at Ernest.

"That's all then," returned Ernest shortly. "Mr. Smith, you settle with him—to ensure what I ask."

Whereupon Ernest stalked past Siebert out into the hall. "Wait outside for me, Hawk."

As once before, Ernest found the door of Anne's room unlocked. He went in and shut it behind him, and proceeded to the bed where she lay, face down, her red hair tumbling about her like fire, her graceful body relaxed.

"Anne," he called, trying to control his voice a moment longer.

She stirred, she turned. Great tragic eyes transfixed him.

"So—this is your revenge?" she whispered hoarsely.

"Yes."

"You fooled me?"

"I did indeed."

She rose to a half-sitting posture, so that the afternoon sunlight, filtering through foliage and window shone on her pale agonized face.

"You—you took your opportunity—you let me believe—you made me love you—you *married* me—you even—even took me as your wife—all for revenge?"

Ernest parried that question by asking one himself. He dared no longer risk this delicious proof of her love, her abasement.

"Anne, did I make you love me?"

"Yes, heaven help me, you did. But don't be mean enough to gloat over me heah. I—I've deserved this."

He walked round the bed and sat down beside her. Taking her hand, he swiftly slipped two rings on her third finger.

"There! There's some more of my revenge!"

She stared uncomprehendingly. But the pallor of her face receded in a wave of color.

"Anne, darling," he whispered, stealing an arm around her. "I've settled with your dad. No fuss, no trouble, He took me up pronto. There'll be no disgrace, no publicity. He is welcome to his ranch in New Mexico."

"Iowa! What—what—" she faltered.

"Say, you're a 'turrible dumbhaid,' to use Nebraskie's words," chided Ernest, as she broke off. "For a girl who has made as many conquests as you have—you're being pretty dense right now."

"But—your revenge?"

"Revenge. What for?"

"For my hateful low-down treatment of you— that killed your love."

"But it didn't, Anne."

"You still—love me?" she whispered. "You are really Ernest Selby—no poor grub-line tenderfoot cowboy after all?"

"Love you. Ha! Ha! That's an understatement. I worship you. Why, all this has turned out wonderfully. You are a true-blue western girl. You proved you loved me, just for myself. Besides that, you're the loveliest girl in all the world. And I'm the luckiest, happiest man in that same world."

"I'm your wife," she breathed.

"Yes, and just as you said, you've become mistress of Red Rock—even if you had to marry the owner."

"Oh!... oh!" she cried, shutting her eyes. Her

face began to change convulsively.

"Kiss me," said Ernest passionately. She kissed him, but it was he who found her lips, and they were quivering.

"Ernest—I—I don't deserve it—I—I don't," she went on brokenly, and then bursting into tears she fell back upon the bed, her face hidden in the pillow.

"Darling, there's nothing to cry over," began Ernest, and then let off, realizing that perhaps there was a good deal. He stroked the shining mass of red hair.

"Well, honey, you have a good cry, if you want," he said rising. "I'll go out and fire that bunch of cowboys."

As he went out he found the living room empty, be he heard Smith and Hepford in the office, the door of which was shut. Hawk waited for him outside, and Daisy, with her father nervously paced the porch.

"Come on, all of you. See the fun," called Ernest, gaily. And he led them at no slight pace around the house and through the pine woods.

"What you up to, boy?" drawled Hawk, half anxiously.

"You mustn't miss this," replied Ernest.

"Wal, Dais an' me air tryin' darn hard to miss nothin', but if you ask me we're shore plumb mysticated," added Brooks.

Soon they reached the bunkhouse where the cowboys stood and sat around. Their former lethargy had vanished. Ernest, leading his little band, halted before them.

"Say, you punchers, do you recollect that when Hawk and I got fired your pard Hyslip made us walk off this ranch?" demanded Ernest.

Shep Davis was cool and civil enough to reply: "Shore, we recollect that."

"Well, was it regular or a low-down trick?"

"Reckon it was low-down all right."

"Listen then," went on Ernest, after an impressive pause, during which four pairs of eyes stared intently at him. "For my part I think you're pretty much of a no-good quartet. But Hawk swears it was Hyslip that spoiled you. So does Nebraskie. I'm willing to give you the benefit of the doubt. . . . Would you rather pack up and walk off this ranch, as Hawk and I did, or apologize to me and swear you'll be better fellows, and stay on here at higher wages?"

Nothing could have been clearer than the fact that those four astounded cowboys thought Ernest was crazy.

"Boys, wake up," added Hawk. "This is the new owner of Red Rock Ranch—Ernest Howard Selby."

Davis was the first to recover. He leaped up, his dark face brightening, and he made a move as if to offer his hand, but on second thought withdrew it.

"Hawk, I might hev knowed . . . . Mr. Selby, I ain't so low-down but what I appreciate a man. I'll accept your offer an' shore reckon I can answer for my pards."

Just then Nebraskie came stamping out on the porch, his cherubic face expressive of his wonderment.

"Whatinhell's goin' on out heah?" he demanded. "Somebody's loco shore."

Ernest actually leaped to confront him.

"Shut up. You're fired!"

"Huh?" ejaculated Nebraskie.

"You're fired."

"Who's firin' me?"

"I am."

"You. . . . My Gawd! Dais—Hawk, the pore boy has gone dotty."

"You're fired, you long lean wild eyed bridegroom," shouted Ernest, warming to the enjoyment of this moment. "Pack up and rustle. You're fired . . . . But you're hired again. You're a partner with Sam Brooks and me in the new development of Red Rock Ranch."

Nebraskie was past speech. He gazed stupidly from Ernest to Hawk. That worthy laughed.

"Nebraskie, let me introduce you to the new owner of Red Rock—Ernest Howard Selby."

A full moment passed in silence while Nebraskie looked from one friend to another.

"It's true. Nebraskie, pard," added Ernest. "Now, you and Dais go home pronto. Pack up for that honeymoon. We leave tomorrow for California."

Ernest turned away from that radiantly happy visage, and as he leaped off the porch he bumped into Daisy. Her face was so rapt that he stopped to plant a kiss full on her smiling lips. Then he rushed toward his ranch house and as he hurried back to his wife his ears were assailed by Nebraskie's high tenor voice, that never before had rung with such a

glad, rich note;
> Son-of-a-gun from Ioway
> He stoled my h——heart awa——ay!

THE SECRET OF
QUAKING ASP CABIN

Log cabins have played a great part in the history of the West. The lonely deserted ones and those falling to ruin, with which any hunter is familiar, have always fascinated me. Many stories of mine tell the romance and drama of these wilderness homes.

Late one autumn afternoon I found myself lost in the forest. This had happened to me before, but not often enough to make the experience something all in the day's hunt. Hours before, the hounds had trailed a bear down over the Mogollon Rim into a canyon. My companions became separated from me. Probably they had followed the cowboys. Already that day I had had two ringing runs after these range riders. The lowering weather threatened rain. I rode along the Rim listening to the bay of the hounds and looking out over that vast green gulf called the Tonto Basin, the wildest and roughest region in Arizona. In case the pack jumped the bear I stood as good a chance as anyone to get a shot.

A cold wind began to blow from the north and the clouds darkened. It grew hard to hear the hounds or an occasional yell of a cowboy. Eventually all sounds of the chase ceased. I turned back on the trail toward camp, keeping a sharp lookout for deer and turkeys.

The Mogollon Rim is an extraordinary geological fault which zigzags three hundred miles across Arizona into New Mexico. It has an altitude close to nine thousand feet and breaks off sheer down into the Tonto Basin. In the other direction it slopes for sixty miles to merge into the desert. The singular feature is that all water runs away from the Rim. Canyons and ridges, like the grooves and ribs of a washboard, head at the Rim and run down. All this region is densely timbered with spruce, pine and aspen.

A flock of wild turkeys lured me off the trail. I chased them for a mile or more down in the woods, without getting a shot. Then fresh deer signs augmented my excitement and drew me on. When I heard elk bugling below I descended the ridge after them. The piercing bugle of a bull elk is one of the wildest and most beautiful calls in nature. Once down off the ridge into the canyon I ascertained that the elk were moving from the north. The herd evidently was small, comprising some cows and yearlings, with at least two bulls.

Most of these canyons, some distance down from the Rim, opened out into grassy parks; I rode into one just in time to see a great tawny elk, with antlers like the roots of an up-turned stump, glide into the pines.

They climbed the ridge and I followed. I did not need to trail them because every little while the leader bugled. Presently an answer pealed from above, and if I needed any more to whet my hunting instinct that was it.

I pursued this band of elk over the ridge, down into another canyon, up again, and on and on, until I discovered that they had either heard or scented me, and after the habit of elk, were just moving along. But it was not this that brought me up with a start. A fine rain had begun to fall; the sky was dark and gave not the slightest hint of the sun. Under such circumstances it was easy for anyone to become lost. I turned back with some concern, until I ascertained the north from moss on a pine; then I turned east. Back-trailing my own tracks would have been futile, for the day was far spent, and I had traveled miles from the Rim. The thing to do was to head east, up and down the ridges, until I crossed Beaver Canyon, in which our camp was located.

If I did come across a landmark that should have been familiar the rain deceived me. All the parks, trees, slopes and ridges looked exactly alike. I was lost, and as the shadows began trooping down the aisles of the forest I decided to find a place to camp, before darkness overtook me. On the morrow, if the sun shone enough to give me my direction, I could get out easily.

Shortly after that decision I came to the brow of a ridge from which I gazed down into a small park, perhaps a score or more acres in extent. On the far side, at the base of the slope, I could see a log cabin, sitting black and strange against the golden blaze of quaking asps. A vacant and eye-like door peered up at me forbiddingly.

The park, with its lonesome manifestation that

someone had lived there sometime, was a welcome sight. I found a dim grass-grown trail leading down. My horse, White Stockings, snorted his approval of the green-carpeted pasture. I heard running water.

It appeared that the old log cabin sat back against a lichened cliff from the tip of which hung wet ferns and scarlet-leaved vines. The roof of split shakes was intact and covered by a thick layer of moss and pine needles. I dismounted and walked around, thrilled by the place. From under the base of the cliff boiled a magnificent spring, ten feet wide and as deep. It was the source of the brook I had forded. One of the most superb silver spruce trees that I had ever seen towered over the cabin with its top above the cliff. To the left and verging right on the west side of the cabin was a grove of quaking asps, that even in the rain and gathering twilight blazed white and gold. Every leaf quaked as if still alive and shuddering in a last agony.

This struck me so singularly, even in that moment of satisfaction at my prospective shelter for the night, that I looked again and gazed long. Aspen trees in the fall are remarkably beautiful. They were my favorites of the high timber belts. But somehow my reaction was not as usual.

Unsaddling my horse, I haltered him with a long lasso to a bush which marked a luxuriant grass plot, and packed my saddle, blankets, canteen and rifle to the cabin. I carried them in and deposited them upon the floor. This proved to be an exception to the majority of cabins I had entered. It had been built of rough-hewn boards and was still solid. A strong odor of bear mingled with the musty scent of dust and pine. The single room was about twenty feet square, with a fireplace and chimney of yellow rock built against the west wall. Here too my quick survey grasped a good job of masonry, still intact except for crumbling corners of the fireplace.

My need was a fire for light and warmth. It behooved me to rustle dry wood while I could see to find it. There was a loft half across the ceiling and a ladder flat against the wall led up to it. I thought I might tear out some of the poles. But I found an old built-in bedstead of peeled poles in a corner, and it was covered with a layer of pine needles. From here the smell of bear emanated pungently. My hand found a round depression where bruin had made his bed. I did not relish the idea of a grizzly returning home to find his bed occupied. But there was no help for it. Only a mean bear would resent my occupancy.

In another corner I found a pile of kindling and pine cones, as dry as tinder.

"All set!" I soliloquized with satisfaction, wondering who had gathered that firewood and how long ago.

Soon I had a fire blazing on the hearth, and it made a vast difference. I went outside and filled my canteen with water from the spring. It was as cold as ice, and like all the water in that wonderful region came from snow water running through granite. I had in my coat a big sandwich—a biscuit with a generous slice of venison. Also I had a piece of chocolate, but this I chose to save for the next day.

Sitting in front of the warm fire, I made my supper and it was sufficient. After that I put on more wood and dried my coat and saddle blankets, upon which I had been sitting. Once more warm and dry, with hunger and thirst satisfied, I felt comfortable. Nevertheless, as one might have supposed, I was neither tired nor sleepy. Furthermore the old cabin intrigued me so thrillingly at first, and then, as I began to study its features and to think, so peculiarly, that I marveled greatly and sought to analyze the reason. It was already a foregone conclusion that I would put this cabin in one of my stories. Strange to record, I never did until now, and I am sure when this is read my readers will not wonder.

By the light of the fire I made out details. The cabin was very old, but as it had been remarkably well and solidly built, it had withstood the ravages of time. There were many signs of dry rot, of crumbling chimney, of general disintegration. In some places the clay that had been used to fill the chinks between the logs was still there, shrunken and as hard as rock. I found indecipherable lettering on the irregular-shaped flat stone above the fireplace, and the imprint of a bloody hand, and bullet holes in the logs. These, however, could hardly account altogether for the powerful curiosity and emotion that stirred in me. I analyzed it presently as a kind of intuitive realization of the life, the drama, the tragedy that had abided there. No old cabin I ever entered, even those down in the Basin, on the scene of that most desperate and bloody feud, the war of the sheepmen and cattlemen fought to the last man, had affected me so poignantly as this one. Surprised and perturbed, I put that down as stress from the excitement of being lost, and I sought to make light of it. But I could not, and in view of what I learned later this was no wonder.

With my saddle for a pillow, and lying between warm blankets, I stretched out to make a night of rest and sleep. While the fire burned I lay awake. The flickering shadows from the changing blaze wrote stories on the gloomy walls of that cabin. When the light waxed dim and failed I shut my eyes. The oppression in my breast persisted. Rain pattered softly on the roof. Alone in that speaking solitude, I surrendered to the phantasms induced by the mystery of what had happened there. It was the prerogative of a writer, but it was not a happy one this night.

I fell asleep. Late in the night I awoke. The radium hands on my watch told two o'clock. Presently I ascertained that the rain had ceased. A wind had arisen and the air was colder. This augured well for my finding my way to camp on the morrow. But the moan and sough and mourn of that wind added to the weird and inexplicable something which pervaded the old cabin. Always as a child I had been afraid of the dark. Even since I had attained manhood, night had always been invested with phantoms, peopled with spirits, full of queer dreams that the sunlight of day dispelled. The conflict between my imagination and my will ended as such conflicts always end, with a victory for the former. Fear of the unknown beset me. I knew perfectly well that I was in no danger physically. But the mind is strange. No scientist or psychologist has plumbed it yet. I was at the mercy of the life, the birth and death, the love and hate and passion, the terror and the ghastliness, of all that had happened in that old cabin. Even if I had never learned what it had all been I would have known it instinctively just the same. Those hours before the gray of dawn were bad ones from the point of view of peace and sleep.

Day broke at last, I got up to pack my things outside. The morning was clear. Frost whitened the grass of the park. The nipping air had teeth. When I got White Stockings saddled and bridled my fingers stung. A rosy light over the high horizon gave me the east, from which I took my direction, and by two hours later, I rode out of the colored forest into the Rim trail, from which I could see the blue haze of the Basin. How good it was to find myself again! But that somber something did not leave me. In two hours and a half I cut off the Rim trail down into Beaver Canyon, and soon rode into camp.

Babe Haught, my old bear hunter, and the Japanese cook, Takahashie, were the only ones in camp. Haught's four sons, the cowboys, and my brother were out hunting for me.

"Wal, I wasn't worried atall," said Babe, his craggy face wreathed in a smile. "Unless you get ketched in a storm, gettin' lost heah don't amount to shucks. All you got to do is foller canyon or ridge up to the Rim."

In some detail I told Haught where I had been and especially about the old cabin.

"Say, you was lost," he replied in surprise. "Thet park's way down, ten miles an' more from the Rim, west of Leonard Canyon. Rough jasper of a country without bein' lost."

"I'll say it's rough. Babe, do you know anything about that old cabin, who lived there—and what might have happened?"

Haught gave his short dry laugh. "Reckon I do. Quakin'-Asp Cabin, it's known to us. Built long before I come to the Tonto, twenty-four years ago. Haven't hunted thar these last half-dozen years. You know the Apaches used to burn the grass over this woods every fall. That made fine open huntin'. But it's growed up brushy. Them jack-pine thickets are shore tough."

"Quaking-Asp Cabin?" I echoed ponderingly. "Babe, didn't a lot happen there?"

"Hell, yes! ... It's haunted—that cabin—Sumthin turrible happened to everyone who lived thar."

"All right, old-timer. Get going," I said with elation.

"Wal, first thing that comes to mind," replied Haught reminiscently, as he squatted down to get a red ember from the campfire to light his pipe, "was told me by Ben Kettle, a hunter heraboots. Ben camped at Quakin'-Asp one night with a feller named Bates, a sheepman. Durin' the night Ben was waked up by a squall from his pardner. One of them coyote-bitten skunks—you know, the kind that have hydrophobia—had hold of Bate's nose. Funny how them poison varmints always bite a feller with a big nose. Ben had to choke the skunk to death to make it let go. Wal, Bates didn't go to see no doctor. He wasn't worried none by them civet-cats. Some days after that, over on the Cibeque at a round, he was took down with rabies. My brother, Henry, was thar an' helped tie Bates in a wagon. They took him to Winslow, whar he had to be roped to a bed. He went mad. Turned black all over. An' he died a horrible death . . . I've knowed of several other fellows bein' bit by hydrophobia skunks . . ."

"Tell more about Quaking-Asp Cabin," I interposed. "That's got me, Haught, I'm on the trail of something."

"Ahuh? Wal, if you trail all thet's come off at Quakin'-Asp, you'll make tracks till doomsday . . . Lemme see. Next I remember thet aboot the Hashknife outfit. More'n twenty years ago. Thet outfit, if I never told you before, was one of Arizonie's best cow outfits. Jim Davis owned it, an' was runnin' ten thousand haid of cattle flanked with thet Hashknife brand. Lefty Dagg, son of the Dagg who was first to be killed in thet Pleasant Valley War old one-arm Matt Taylor told you aboot, was foreman of this outfit. Wal, Jim Davis an' his bunch camped thar at Quakin'-Asp one day in the fall of thet year. Jim had been to Pine, where he'd sold a big herd of stock to the Mormons. He had a wad of money on him, an' Dagg with his cowboys was well-heeled. Naturally they fell to gamblin' an' from thet to fightin'. Dagg killed a cowboy Davis set much store on an' it riled the boss. Nobody ever knowed for shore the truth of what come off. They said on the range thet it was an even break an' they said also thet Dagg murdered Davis. We never got the straight of thet. But we did find out, you bet, thet Dagg an' his outfit went crooked after thet fight. They turned rustlers. In the years thet follered the Hashknife earned a hard name. They fought other cattle outfits. But it was fightin' among themselves that snuffed thet outfit out. Thar has been a dozen Hashknife outfits since, an' all of them took on two or three guntoters from the older outfit, which I reckon worked like a few rotten apples on a barrel of good ones. No Hashknife outfit has ever outlived thet heritage."

"Babe, that's good—a whole story in itself. But not the one I'm on the track of," I replied eagerly. "Go on."

"Wal, the first time I rode down to Quakin'-Asp Cabin I had a jar," resumed Haught. "Thar was a feller livin' thar alone, a lean, dark-browned man with 'range rider' stamped all over him. Thet was twenty-three years ago, but I remember as well as if it was yestiddy. 'Cause thet hombre throwed his gun on me an' I had a hell of a time talkin' him out of borin' me. But I convinced him thet even if he was on the dodge he needn't fear me. I stayed all night with him an' he waxed friendly. Before I left he omitted tellin' me his name but he did tell me that there was a price on his haid. The next summer when I rode in thar again he was gone. I never saw him again. But years afterward a rich an' respected cattleman told on his deathbed a story that went the rounds heah in Arizonie. I figgered thet he an' the outlaw I had met at Quakin'-Asp had been pards, ridin' together in the same outfit. They both fell in love with the ranchman's daughter. He hisself had pulled the crooked deal thet his pard took the guilt for an' he couldn't die with it on his conscience. He told his old friend's name an' begged him to come an' stand free before the world. But the outlaw had long gone crooked of his own account. If he ever heahed of his pard's confession no one knowed. He was shot in a road-agent hold-up in New Mexico."

"Babe, you're hot on the track of what I felt that night in haunted Quaking-Asp Cabin," I declared forcibly. "Come on. Come on."

"Wal, I dunno aboot that," replied the old bear hunter dubiously. Then he told me the story of Tappan and his great burro Jennie.

Tappan had been a giant prospector, a wanderer of the wasteland, a lonely hermit whose young manhood and maturity had been given to the naked shingles and rocky fortresses of the desert, to the lure of gold. One time, way down on the barrens at the base of the Chocolate range in California, his burro gave birth to a little one that Tappan feared he would have to kill. But it chanced that when he was about to rid the mother of her encumbrance he stumbled upon the richest pocket of gold he had ever found. He spared the life of the baby burro and called her Jennie. She grew to be the largest and finest and most intelligent burro that Tappan had ever owned. She became famous on the desert from Picacho to Death

Valley. Other prospectors tried to buy her and steal her. But Jennie grew to be more than gold to Tappan.

Once Tappan was caught in one of the terrible storms of flying poison dust, and torrid blasts of heat that prevail in Death Valley in summer. At midnight the hellish furnace winds began to blow. Blinded, lost, Tappan clung to the tail of his faithful burro, and she led him up and out of the valley of death and desolation. After that Tappan loved Jennie more than all the burros he had ever owned.

Tappan's peculiar thirst for gold led him in quest of all the lost gold mines that the desert fact and legend had left to torture prospectors. The day inevitably came when he took the trail of the famed and elusive Lost Dutchman Mine somewhere far into the wilds of the Superstitions in Arizona.

One night into his camp rode a group of riders, four men and one woman. They were not welcome, because Tappan had bags of gold and preferred to be lonely, but the fair-spoken leader, who claimed his band was lost and hungry, and the persuasive offices of the handsome young woman, prevailed upon Tappan to be hospitable.

There had been no woman in Tappan's life. This one contrived to win his sympathy. She claimed to be virtually a prisoner and she hated her captivity. She worked upon the mind and heart of the simple prospector.

The leader of the band talked about the ranch he had up in the timbered canyons of the Tonto Basin, and what a contrast the shady cool retreat, the singing brook, the richness of verdure and toothsomeness of venison and turkey, made to this ghastly desert of cactus and rock, down upon which the pitiless summer sun had begun to burn. Before Tappan lay down to sleep that night the woman had won him to go with them. She hinted that he might save her.

Ten long days Tappan rode with the gang, on one of their horses, while Jennie plodded behind, loaded with his pack. They climbed to a canyon up under the gold rim of the Mogollon. The ranch and cattle did not materialize, but all the other features the leader had lauded to Tappan were there in abundance. Tappan reveled in all the rich attributes of that timbered canyon, so different from his desert. Then he fell in love with the woman Bess. It was a malady that he could not resist nor cure. Not until afterward did it occur to Tappan how strange that the men left him so much alone with Bess. And when she confessed her love he lived in his first fool's paradise.

Bess confessed that her associates were rustlers and she begged Tappan to save her from them, to take her far away and make her happy. Tappan consented to that in the only transport of his life. They planned to ride away early one night, but it would be impossible to take Jennie. To part with his faithful burro, to betray her for this woman, to leave her alone, knowing she would wait there for him until she died, filled Tappan's heart with anguish. But it had to be done.

They escaped one night on horseback, with only one pack animal, carrying Tappan's bags of gold, some food and bedding. They rode south all night and all the next day before resting. Tappan believed they were safe, but Bess showed fear of pursuers. While they were eating at their campfire, something stampeded their horses. Tappan went to hunt them and succeeded in catching only one. Upon his return to camp he found Bess gone with his bags of gold. She left a note swearing she loved Tappan and would have gone to hell for him, but this was the only way she could save his life.

Tappan tracked that gang out of Arizona, down through California into Mexico. The blue-eyed woman and the swarthy leader who gambled and drank at every town made them easy to trail. One by one the other members of the gang disappeared. At length Tappan stood bowed over Bess's grave and he buried his love and heart there with her. And soon after that he got his great hands on the villain who had murdered her—the suave leader of the rustler gang—to break his bones and wring his neck.

Tappan retraced his steps. A year and more had passed. He remembered Jennie and he journeyed across the desert wastes, far up into Arizona, to the green and gold canyon where he had deserted her. To his everlasting relief and joy he found her there, waiting for him, as she had waited a thousand and more mornings on the desert. Tappan took her to the nearest hamlet and there spent his remaining gold for an outfit. Packing her more heavily than ever before, Tappan turned his back forever on the desert and climbed up over the Rim to wander down into the shady canyons and shining parks until he happened upon Quaking-Asp Cabin. There he took up his abode for the summer and fall.

But he lingered late, loath to leave this verdant, colorful retreat, the only one that had ever wholly satisfied him.

Then one day a man on foot strode upon Tappan as he sat in his doorway. This intruder claimed to be lost and hungry. Tappan guessed him to be a bad man, hunted surely, and not to be trusted. But as Tappan now had nothing to lose he arose to take the fugitive in and feed him, hoping he would be on his way next day. But Blade, as he called himself, did not leave. He stayed, day after day, though Tappan offered to see him off with a share of his diminishing store of food. Blade feared he could not find his way out of that wilderness alone, and always he tried to persuade Tappan to go. His argument was that they must start before the snow fell. If they were snowed in there they would starve to death.

But Tappan, grown surly and resentful, stayed on, until a great howling blizzard blew down upon the park. When the storm passed there were four feet of snow on the level. Winter had set in. Tappan saw the peril he would not think of before. While waiting for a crust to harden on the snow, he fashioned snowshoes. The day came. Blade raged at Tappan's intention to take Jennie with him. He argued in vain. Then in a passion he snatched up Tappan's rifle to kill the burro.

"We'll need the meat," he yelled.

"Wha-at! Eat my burro! My Jennie!" roared

Tappan, and made at this man.

A terrific fight for the rifle ensued. Blade was big and powerful, but no match for the giant prospector. They fought to and fro in front of Quaking-Asp Cabin, treading the snow down, while Jennie watched meekly. At last the rifle broke in their hands, Blade getting the stock and Tappan the barrel. Tappan warded off blows until he had his opening. He brained his opponent. Blade fell back in a snowbank, his boots sticking out grotesquely.

"Huh! You would eat my burro!" Tappan grunted, and binding his wounds he strapped a tarpaulin and his meager remnant of food upon Jennie. Then on snowshoes he set out leading the burro.

Jennie's sharp little hoofs broke through the snow crust, but not all four at once. Tappan climbed up on the ridge when the crust was harder. He headed downhill. That night he ate and slept under a spruce. All day he led Jennie, plodding along, zigzagging the slopes. Night passed and another day and another night. His food gave out. Jennie nibbled at the buck-brush and other greenery. Tappan lost track of time. When the snow began to thin out and soften he put Jennie on the tarpaulin and dragged her along. Tappan passed out of the spruce, down out of the pines, down into the cedars. At sunset one day he gazed down upon the open range, bare of snow in spots. Spent and tottering, Tappan fell upon the tarpaulin and covered himself. The night down at the edge of the open desert was bitterly cold. Tappan slept. In the morning when Jennie welcomed the sunrise with a long drawn "Hee-haw, hee-haw, hee-hawee," and waited for Tappan, he did not awaken.

"Thet's the way it always seemed to me," concluded the old backwoods storyteller. "Shore I can't prove it all happened thet way. But Blade's skeleton was found, his skull split. An' then aboot the same time next summer, the riders found all the coyotes had left of Tappan. Jennie roamed thet sage an' cedar range for years, wilder'n any wild deer. Men who knowed Tappan's story an' who're still livin' saw Tappan's burro after she grew wild. But I never saw her."

"Great stuff, Babe!" I exclaimed, shaken to my depths. "But still that's not it. That's not all. Who built Quaking-Asp Cabin? What happened there first, before all these things you tell of?"

"Wal, I reckon thar's only one man left in these parts who can tell you if anyone knows. Thet's old one-arm Matt Taylor. Mebbe you can get him het up to talk, like you did aboot the sheep war."

After our hunt ended and we got down to the little Tonto settlement I went to call on Matt Taylor. But he was away somewhere. The following fall on the way in I tried again, with like result. Then twice during that hunt I endeavored to find Quaking-Asp Cabin, once alone, and another time with Haught's son. We failed to locate the park. All this vain search only whetted my appetite for that story. The longer I had to wait the bigger it loomed.

The third season after my discovery of Quaking-Asp Cabin I met a half-breed Indian, an intelligent fellow and a great hunter, and invited him to my camp. It turned out that my bear hunters had no use for him. They were jealous no doubt, as he was the most unerring rifle shot in that region, and I had taken a decided fancy to him. The fact that he had killed a couple of men and was a sort of desperado did not influence me greatly. He was the grandest fellow to hunt with that I ever had with me. He rode a mule that could hear and scent and see game quicker than any hunter—but that is another story.

This half-breed led me straight across country, over ridge and down canyon, to Quaking-Asp Cabin. Early in October the park and wooded slopes presented a glorious blend of autumn colors. It was without doubt the most idyllic and lovely spot I ever encountered in any forest.

I rode down ahead of my guide, and along the edge of the park, where isolated pines and spruce and aspens straggled out toward the open. A troop of deer trotted away under the trees, and turned to watch me, with long ears erect. Quick as a flash I piled off my horse, and picking out a four-point buck I let him have it in the breast. Making a prodigious leap, with front feet doubled under him, he crashed down into the brush. His action indicated a mortal wound. In my hunter's excitement at downing so fine a buck, the first in two seasons, I ran forward. Coming upon him I stood my rifle against a sapling, and drawing my hunting knife I was about to step to him when he gave a bound right at me.

His hindquarters were down and he had leaped upon me on his front feet. Surprise checked me and then horror rooted me to the spot. My bullet had gone through the deer, destroying the power of his hindquarters. He presented a bloody and terrible sight. With his last power of movement he meant to kill me. All dying beasts of the wild at bay exhibit eyes almost too appalling for the gaze of man. I was sick, frozen, paralyzed. That buck lowered his sharp antlers to rip me asunder when a rifle cracked and he fell in a heap. My guide had come upon me in my predicament and had shot from his horse.

"Never go close to a dying deer!" he admonished.

I pulled myself together, but the incident spoiled my return to Quaking-Asp Cabin. It fit in with all the rest I had felt about that lovely strange place. I rested while the Indian cut out two haunches of the deer and packed them in his slicker. Then we walked on to the cabin, leading our horses. A reluctance to enter the cabin held me back. But my guide glided around with a somber mien that struck me most singularly. It dawned upon me that he knew the place—that it meant a great deal to him—but the effect upon him was far from happy. This slowly stirred my old curiosity. My thirst for the romance or tragedy, whatever haunted the spot, returned stronger than ever.

He came at length to sit beside me in the golden shade of the aspens. For a man who was half Indian his strong face appeared less bronze than usual. Beads of sweat stood out upon his brow, and his dark eyes burned with a somber and inscrutable fire.

"Haven't been here for nigh on twenty years. Same as ever." he muttered, as if to himself.

"You must have been only a kid then?" I queried, feeling my way.

"No, I was a man then . . . How old do you reckon me?"

"About twenty-eight, maybe thirty," I ventured.

"I'm close to fifty . . . Do you know, sir, I wouldn't have come here for any man in the world but you?"

"Indeed! Well, thanks very much, my hunter pard. I sure appreciate that," I replied feelingly. "But why such reluctance? It's such a wonderful place to me."

"I was born here," he replied huskily, and hung his dark hawklike head.

It was not that astounding information which shocked the blood back to my heart, but a flash of intuition that at last I was on the heels of the tremendous secret of Quaking-Asp Cabin.

"Born here?" I ejaculated wonderingly. "Haught didn't tell me that."

"He doesn't know it."

"Oh! . . . Look here . . . For three years I've been trying to find out all about this Quaking-Asp Cabin. Old Matt Taylor, who told me the story of TO THE LAST MAN, is the only one, Haught says, who knows what happened here. I've been trying to meet him again. . . . But, maybe now, I won't need to, if you . . . "

"Old Matt worked here when I was a boy. He's over eighty now and his memory is failing . . . I'll tell you who built this cabin—what happened in it—why a shadow hangs over it."

"You'll never be sorry,' I rejoined with deep gratitude.

"I was born here—played and roamed and hunted—worked here and loved it until *she* died."

"Friend, I'm primed for a great story. I've waited years. But before you start, tell me . . . how does it come that you speak so fluently and well, if it's true, as you told me, you're half Apache, and lived here in this wilderness till you were twenty years old?"

"Sounds queer, but it's simple enough. *Her* mother was from the East. She was educated—taught us both."

"Was *her* mother yours, too?"

"No, mine was Apache. I never was sure which of the brothers was my father. But when my heart broke and the devil came up in me and I drifted from hunter to a hard-nut cowboy, to rustler, and gunman, then I suspected my father was he—the brother who cast the evil spell over this homestead."

Then for hours this somber-eyed white Apache talked, living over the past. What he related would have filled a volume. From all he saw and heard and felt and suffered there I embodied, with the privilege and license of the writer, my own tragic tale of Quaking-Asp Cabin.

Among the passengers on the first Santa Fe train to reach Flagerstown, Arizona, in the seventies, were Richard Starke, his young wife Blue, and his brother Len. They left the train at this town because the wildness of the black timbered mountains all around appeared a refuge for an eloping girl under age and the erring brother, Len, who had fled to escape prison.

The frontier town, with its Indians and cowboys, its brawling streets and noisy gambling hells, was thrillingly new and strange to the Easterners. A vast contrast to conventional Boston! The brothers felt the leap of primitive blood and that the life of adventure they had read and dreamed of as boys was to become a reality.

Richard Starke had been ten years old when his only brother, Len, an unwanted child, had come into the world; and all of Len's nineteen years Richard had loved him, shielded him, and had at last saved the weakling from jail, if not from disgrace. Len was a handsome stripling, careless, lovable, too weak to curb bad instincts. Blue was pretty and spoiled, wild as any schoolgirl, mad with love and freedom from restraint. Richard had converted considerable property into cash, which he carried with him, and which must be carefully conserved to last for years. Long before Richard reached Flagerstown the West had called deeply to him and had claimed him forever. What life he chose must necessarily be Blue's and Len's. There they stood, then, on the wide dusty street of this lawless frontier settlement, like so many thousands of Easterners and Southerners who had journied toward the setting sun, many of them keen to put their shoulders to the wheel of empire, many of them fugitives, outcasts, adventurers, all of them a part of this great movement of an expanding people.

Richard left his wife and brother at the hotel and went up to mingle with the men of Flagerstown. A stranger among a crowd of strangers, he excited no notice, and his queries were the natural ones of a newcomer. The upshot of this contact was that under cover of the darkness of the spring night he drove a team and heavily laden wagon down the lonely road to the south, headed for the wildest section of Arizona. Blue sat beside him, speechless from excitement and rapture. Len lounged at the back, dragging three horses by their halters.

In eight days' travel down toward the Tonto Basin the Starkes passed but two homesteads. The road passed through a virgin forest, its green and brown solemnity broken here and there by grassy parks, where game abounded. At last on the rim of a vast blue basin the homeseekers encountered a road, cut through the forest toward the east. They camped at that intersection, undecided whether to venture along this wild rim, or follow the main road down into this deep mountain-encompassed valley of green and gold.

A caravan of three wagons caught up with them at this camp, and the leader made friends with Richard. He said he was a Mormon and belonged to the little settlement of Pine, down in the basin. It was plain that any new homesteaders traveling this way would be welcome among the Mormons. Richard acknowledged no creed, nor did he frown upon the proselyte's kindly advances. Richard said to him, "Lead me to a secluded place deep in the wilderness. Help me build a log cabin. Sell me stock and things to plant."

Next day the Mormon sent his wagons on, and mounting a horse he led the Starkes all day along that rim road, with the silver-green wall of forest on one side, and the ragged rim and dim blue basin on the other. This road had lately been cut through the forest by General Crook and his soldiers, in their campaign against the Apache Indians.

From that camp on the rim the guide drove Richard's wagon zigzagging down a ridge until the windfalls made further progress on wheels impossible. Then he packed the horses, except the one that Blue was to ride, and led miles and miles down into an ever-increasing wilderness of giant trees and swales and rocky fortresses, at last to come out into an open park, level as a lake, shining like a gun, dotted with wild game, and surrounded by slopes of tufted pine crests and fern-festooned cliffs. A solitude and silence such as these Easterners had not dreamed of lay heavily and sweetly upon the park.

"Here we will live!" said Richard in deep elation.

"Oh, Dick. . . it's paradise!" cried Blue.

Len gazed from a survey of the lovely spot to turn a grateful light of tear dimmed eyes upon the brother who had saved him.

They pitched camp under the great spruce that shaded the spring. The Mormon took the rest of this day packing down the remaining supplies from the wagon. On the following morning he said, "I will go. My sons and I will fetch what you need, and catch timber and throw up your cabin and plant your grain. God abide with you here!"

The days that came passed like magic. They made a pioneer out of Richard Starke. Strong and shapely, skillfully designed and built, the homestead of yellow peeled pine logs went up, back wall against the cliff, stone chimney rising sturdily, at length to send its column of blue smoke lazily aloft to mingle with the green foliage. The brown tilled park, rich with its many fallow years, grew green with beans and maize and cabbage and turnips, and with the orchard and vineyard transplanted from Pine. Calves bawled in the white aspen-pole pens; chickens learned to run from the shadows of swooping hawks; the bray of burros mingled with the bugle of elk.

Blue was rapturously happy despite the housewifely duties so difficult for her. Richard had encouraged an Apache family to stay and live in the canyon at the head of the park. And the Mormons left one of their number, Matthew Taylor, a young farmer and experienced hunter, to help the Starkes. Len Starke hated work and he ran wild in the woods, along the trout brooks. The frosty autumn days, with their colored falling leaves, saw Len roaming the forest with the buckskin-clad Taylor, and that season brought up the one unplumbed strong instinct in him.

When snow fell Taylor and the Indians went back down into the basin for the winter. But for the Starkes, to be snowed in meant only a climax to their adoption by the wilderness. With cords of firewood, meat hanging under the eaves, stored fruit and vegetables, books and light and warmth, they welcomed the roar of the north wind in the pines and the white drifting clouds of snow.

Winter passed and spring returned. Matt Taylor came back with the Apaches. That summer saw Letith, the daughter of the Apache squaw, develop from a child to a slim, voluptuous creature, dusky-eyed, wild as a deer, restless at her work, shy before the bold-eyed Len, ever running from him only to be pursued.

Richard worked in the fields. He had grown to love this park and cabin. His cattle had begun to multiply. He would prosper here. And as the months passed, dread of that reaching hand from out of the East gradually folded its sable coat and faded away.

Another golden-scarlet Indian summer merged into white winter. At nineteen Blue had outgrown her girlish frailty. Outdoors three-fourths of the year, she had grown strong and brown and beautiful. Richard reached the summit of his fullness of joy. His sacrifice had been rewarded. Blue seemed to be changing, growing. Len was content with his lonely fishing, hunting, dreaming. The future held prospects beyond a lonely seclusion. The snow fell and melted, and again it was summer.

While Richard was absent, having gone to Pine to pack up supplies, during one of Taylor's frequent trips to the railroad, the Indian girl Letith gave birth to a baby boy. This happened in Richard's cabin, where Blue had kept the girl for her confinement. Len swore that the baby was not his. Letith did not betray him in words, but her great dusky eyes, fixed upon Len with the strange worship of the savage maiden for the white man, appeared to be conclusive evidence for Richard.

Blue repudiated his opinion with a passion that amazed him. But presently when Letith's father dragged her away, leaving the baby there, Blue took it to her heart, and seemed all at once to blossom into a woman. When Blue's daughter, Hillie, was born the following summer, Richard accepted the idea of adopting the Apache maiden's boy.

Then the threatening shadow that had revived in Richard's mind, to haunt him again with its mocking inevitableness, retreated with a subtle and welcome change in Len. The boy seemed to be growing into a man, and up until the hunting season that year he worked hard around the ranch. What with these precious truths, and the multiplying cattle and the mounting grain, Richard was too busy working and being happy to count the months until they had grown into years. Also these same things, added to his loving faith, blinded him to what he came bitterly to learn.

One day in midautumn he was up in the woods with Matt Taylor rounding up calves that had become too numerous to brand. Something, he forgot afterward what, gave him occasion to make a short cut on foot down the slope to the park, at a point near the cabin. As he was about to emerge from the wooded slope to enter the straggling spruces and aspens he heard Blue's high sweet laughter ringing out, with a rich bell-like note he had never heard. She came in sight running, looking back, her eyes wide and dark, her breasts shaking under her thin garment. She hid behind a tent-shaped spruce that spread its lower branches on the ground. Then Len appeared, flushed of face, his hair disheveled, his eyes shooting ardent flames everywhere. He found Blue. She had only run to be pursued, only hidden to be found. Len seized her with a low exultant cry, and as he enveloped her tightly her arms slid up his shoulders to clasp round his neck. That moment, so shockingly fraught with amaze and panic, froze Richard in his tracks. And the next, when his brother's handsome rosy face bent to his wife's, and their lips came together, and she stood tense, her eyelids closed heavy and rapt, was one in which Richard's heart broke, and a horrible hell bellowed into his soul.

It was Len who broke that embrace, not Blue. She clung to him as they wended a slow way back to the cabin. The children were playing and shrieking around the door. Richard watched the lovers enter and stood stricken until he saw Blue's scarlet face flash against the blackness of the open doorway. She peered out into the park, then disappeared.

Richard plunged up the slope like a mortally wounded bull and at length slunk under a dense spread of spruce to lie like a log. When, hours or minutes later, his mind awoke to clear thought again, he saw the catastrophe. He understood then the change in Len—his staying at home, his frenzied labors, his unusual gaiety. He understood Blue's glamorous beauty, the pale glow of her face, the silver music of her laughter, the moods that alternated in her. He recalled now the look he had seen in Len's bold eyes, across the cabin room, in the firelight. He recalled his wife meeting him in the door, at his return from work, too innocent-eyed, too sweet and loving to be true. Len and Blue had fallen in love, terribly, not as boy and girl, but as man and woman.

The husband reasoned that they had only recently discovered their love, that they had just begun to surrender to the ectasy of it, and not yet wholly and shamelessly. Richard had to save them. But how? He could not send Len adrift, after all these years of protection, to become an outcast among the vicious characters of the Basin. He would have to hide from Blue his knowledge of her duplicity, if that were possible. Still, was it duplicity? Could she help falling in love with his brother, younger, handsomer, wilder? Richard blamed himself. This was the penalty of eloping with a sentimental girl, of forcing her into womanhood. This was the price he had to pay for taking his brother from the world, which would have made him pay for his weaknesses.

Richard plodded down toward the park. It was the hour of sunset in which the golden rays of light shone down upon the manifold autumn hues with a beauty and glory that made this lovely place all satisfying. Richard saw it once more—and saw it die and become transformed with an appalling shadow.

He changed as had the aspect of nature. He went back to the cabin with a gnawing rat in his heart, a burning jealousy, a clouded mind, all at bitter war with his better self. Blue thought he was tired; Len spoke of Matt returning alone from work, and he gave Richard a strange glance. Their gaiety went into eclipse. It never pealed out again in that cabin.

From that hour Richard confined himself to labors in the fields close at hand. He never left the park. And as the fineness of him disintegrated under this wreck of love, so the reaction upon Blue and Len was correspondingly great. The shadow deepened over that household. Len knew that his perfidy had been discovered—that he was permitted to stay on there through the incredible loyalty of his brother. He ceased to work; he roamed the forest; he lay idle and brooding under the spruce; he rode to Pine and came back smelling of rum.

Blue's bloom left her, and so did the dancing light of her violet eyes. She tried to remedy the evil, to get back to Richard, but there was a stronger will than hers at work, a power that dragged her down. Richard divined it was Len's love and Blue's mad response to it that had enslaved her. They never realized, these two misguided and fated lovers, that when Richard plodded the furrows of the fields or stood leaning on his hoe, or sat brooding before the fire at night, that he was fighting himself, his baser physical side, to beat it down and go away forever, leaving them to a possible happiness. But that was what obsessed him. Greater love hath no man! This was triumphing in Richard's soul.

One day in early fall he had gone to the upper end of the park, taking his shotgun with him to kill a grouse or wild turkey. Len had gone hunting early that morning. Taylor was picking beans with Hillie and the Indian boy Starke. Richard avoided passing them. Of late the Mormon had watched him with covert sympathy.

In the aspen swale where the park converged there was a huge pile of dead hardwood that Richard had snaked down to chop up for winter cooking fires. Day after day he had labored at this task, finding mental relief in physical violence. But today, which was to see the fruition of this struggle, he never lifted up the ax. For hours he sat in the melancholy forest, his soul naked to his inner gaze. All around him were the amber and purple blaze of leaves, the passing brown rumps of elk, the frisky gray squirrels, the drumming grouse and scratching turkeys, to which sights and sounds he was oblivious.

Toward sundown he arose like a giant casting off a burden and bent his stride toward the distant cabin, with his mind made up. He would give Blue to his brother with enough money for them to make a new start in life, far away somewhere. But the mother must part with Hillie.

The trail kept to the straggling spruce and pine trees along the edge of the park. Richard had not gone far when a rustling in the brush reminded him that he had not thought of the meat Blue had importuned him to hunt.

His quick glance caught a movement of parting leaves. Then not ten steps distant he saw two round black holes, and he looked along the brown barrels of a shotgun, into the eyes that blazed murderous hate and hell. Len!

The gun belched smoke and fire. A terrific shock knocked Richard flat and his ears clapped with a crash. His faculties sustained a stunning check, but instantly rallied. He lay still, expecting his brother to emerge from the brush to see if he were dead. He heard rustlings and retreating steps.

Richard's effort to sit up ended in a fall. He had tried to use his right arm. It had been blown off with part of his shoulder. Blood poured down his side in a red deluge. He feared part of his lung had been shot away. Something hot and salty welled up into his mouth.

Using his left arm, he got to his knees and began to crawl along the trail toward the cabin. He met the imminence of death with an appalling strength of spirit. He would not die. He would face this perfidious brother who had meant to destroy him. He must look into Blue's eyes to see if she was a party to this lecherous crime. On he crawled, and the colored maple leaves along the trail were the redder for his passing. He reached the corner of the cabin and struggled erect, holding to the logs. Children's mirth struck Richard incongruously. Taylor at the woodpile with axe aloft saw him and stiffened. Richard got to the door—held to the lintel.

Blue appeared inside, her face set, white, strained. Her starting eyes saw first his bloody boots—traveled upward—over his dripping garments—to the gory side with its missing sleeve and arm. They met Richard's gaze. Conscious and insupportable truth gleamed in them. They betrayed the intelligence that he was not dead, but alive. Then they protruded and fixed in horror. She shrieked and fell back into the cabin.

Richard staggered inside. As he lurched for the chair his hand left a perfect crimson imprint upon the yellow stone over the fireplace. Then Taylor rushed in, panting, mute with fright.

"Shot—myself," gasped Richard, and strangling, he succumbed to faintness.

When he recovered consciousness he found himself on the couch along the wall where the light from the door fell. Either his body was bound so tightly that he could scarcely breathe or the excruciating agony made it feel so. Matt Taylor knelt beside him, feeling his pulse.

"Dick," he said hoarsely. "I reckon you'll die—pronto."

Richard's lips framed an almost inaudible "No!"

"Your arm's gone—shoulder—top of your lung! Man, tell me what to do when—when—"

"Matt . . . I'll . . . not die."

"I hope not. But I reckon you will. Did all I could, Dick. Listen, man! What'll I tell—do? . . . I trailed you—found your gun. It hadn't been fired!"

"Tell . . . do . . . nothing."

"Ahuh!" The Mormon's dark and grim glance rested wonderingly upon Richard. "Shall I pray for you?"

"Yes . . . that . . . I live."

This religious Mormon bowed his head over Richard and prayed in husky fervid whisper, the last of which grew intelligible: "And damn their cursed souls to hell!"

"Yes!" whispered Richard, echoing that in his own soul. "Where are they?"

"Outside. Waiting for me to tell them you've passed on."

"Matt—stay by me . . . Give me whiskey—water . . . I shall not die."

Richard knew that nights and days passed, because his consciousness registered light and dark through his closed eyelids. His senses were in the grip of a transcendent and superhuman will. He refused to die. His mind must conquer his body. A terrible and insupportable revenge upon these traitors would be to live. Agony was nothing. Time was nothing. Love would have let him die. But hate would save his life.

The days passed. If Richard could have looked at himself lying prostrate there he would not have seen any perceptible improvement in his condition, but his inward eye told him differently. His spirit swore and his mind believed that it had known beforehand he could have been killed outright and yet would have come back to life.

Often he felt the children near him, and the time came when he opened his eyes and whispered to them. Violet-eyed Hillie, with her curly nut brown hair, was six years old. The Apache boy Starke, Len's son, was seven, a tall lad, inscrutable, fated to tragedy. They both were that. Richard could not resurrect the love he had felt for his little girl.

But when Blue was in the cabin Richard never opened his eyes. Often he heard her and Len whispering outside. They were waiting for him to die.

One night in the gloaming at the end of his belated fall, when the children were asleep, the low voices of the lovers floated to Richard on the still air.

"Matt says Dick will live."

"Oh, I hope to God he will, but I fear he won't," cried Blue poignantly.

"I can't stay here longer, Blue . . . I'm tortured."

"You are tortured! For God's sake, what am I?"

"Let us run away, Blue. You can't stand it either. When you come out of this cabin you look like—death. . . ."

"Yes. Death! There is death in there. All that Dick was! Love, home, child, happiness—dead!"

"But it's too late, Blue . . . We might find those things—somewhere—after we forgot . . . Come. Let's take Hillie and go."

"Oh, how can you? . . . Len, I loved you—love you still. I gave you the best of me—what he never had. I share your guilt. . . . Oh God, help me! My eyes were wide open. If Dick had died I'd have been his murderer, equally with you . . . But now—it's all different. While he lives I must stay here—and suffer—and work my fingers to the bone for him . . . and never dare to look him in the face again!"

"What will become of me?"

"That doesn't matter, any more than what becomes of me. Go away. Leave me peace in retribution . . . But if you have any manhood, you will let this terrible deed—this fruit of our passion—be a turning point in your life."

"Manhood! Am I my brother's keeper? I want you, Blue. You, my woman, else I'll go to hell!"

"Len, if you stayed here, you'd make me loathe you. Leave—while I still love you! Leave me to give my life to him."

"I'll go, you white-livered cheat!" he cried in bitter passion. "It's the end. I knew—I always knew this lonely hole would be our ruin. We were not savages. But we became savages—like that bastard son of mine in there . . . This wilderness cabin is accursed. If it were not cursed by nature, by a primitive something as raw as these yellow logs we threw up, then I cursed it—my crooked, rotten, selfish self—and you cursed it—with your pretense of wifehood and motherhood—with your damned sweet lure—with the female in you that couldn't be satisfied. . . . Good-by, Blue Starke!"

Matt Taylor stayed at the cabin until winter set in and then went out on snowshoes. Richard lay on his couch, sleeping, mending, his mind warped in one narrow orbit. He never spoke to Blue—never looked at her when she might observe it. But he saw her carry water, chop wood, bake and cook and mend, and use what hours these tasks left her to teach the children. What little communication there was between her and him was carried by Hillie, and sometimes by Starke. The Indian boy revealed a somber affection for Richard, and through that long solemn winter Hillie grew to worship him. Richard saw this, marveled that it made no change in him. But he was dead to all save hate. He survived to make this woman suffer, and the days were as moments.

Spring came, and with it Matt Taylor with a pack train of supplies. He said his prayers had been answered. That summer Richard arose from his couch to walk about, a shell of a man, ghastly of visage, marvelously and imperceptibly gaining.

Summer and fall went by, and winter, similar to the preceding one, except that Richard read and brooded before the fire. There was never a moment, waking or sleeping, in which he was not conscious of the tragic presence of his wife. She seemed sustained, too, by a spirit that neither hard work nor misery could break. The measure of her sin was a faithfulness and repentance that came too late. Her beauty augmented, but it was no longer the bloom and freshness of a girl. At twenty-five, all that she had lived, all the havoc she had wrought, all the soul that anguish had burned to gold, showed under the marble of her face, in the terror of wide-open, staring eyes.

When planting season came again Blue worked in the fields, with Hillie and Starke to help. They were springing up like the weeds they had to pull. Taylor came once more with supplies, for which this time he received no recompense. During the succeeding years he visited the cabin every summer, as if the place haunted him, as he said it haunted Len Starke. It was rumored, Taylor said, that Len lived in the forest like an Indian, and cattlemen of the Tonto called him hard names. More than once he had been seen by riders in the vicinity of Quaking-Asp Cabin, by which Richard's home had become known. It was conceivable that the man found an irresistible urge to return to the scene of his great crime, to take a hidden look at the spot which had so fatally influenced his life. Richard did not allow Matt to tell Blue of Len's visits, and in his own mind he sustained a surprise that Len showed character enough to make them. Blue should have no sympathy. There might have been solace in the proof of Len's remembrance, perhaps in the thought that he wanted to see her.

Then Matt Taylor did not visit the park for five years. Sometimes forest riders rode down and in the fall hunters blundered in there, or came out of curiosity. Richard saw that the mystery of Quaking-Asp Cabin was guessed at if not known.

His cattle were rustled or they wandered down into the dense thickets and canyons to be killed by lions and bears, or to become as wild as the beasts that preyed upon them. The once fertile fields of maize and beans returned to grass and weeds again. Richard, like a ghost of his old self, worked desultorily in the little garden that Blue, with Hillie and Starke, planted each summer. Prosperity had long departed and poverty came in the gloomy cabin door.

The Mormon friend rode down again, after his long absence, and stayed in the park awhile. But it was evident that despite his interest in Richard and Blue, and his affection for Hillie and Starke, he could not endure to stay long.

The white winters succeeded the brown autumns, as the summers fled on the heels of spring. Such was the peculiarity of Richard's malady that he did not see the swift flight of time nor the development of the children. He saw only this woman who had laid waste his heart and his life; and the more wretched she became, the more determined he was to survive.

In the spring of the tenth year after the catastrophe, Hillie died. This thing wedged thought and feeling and realization into the almost impenetrable sepulcher of Richard's mind. Death, in a strange flash, brought back his love for his child. She had grown to be a frail girl of sixteen, lovely as one of the columbines under the cliff, and like them shadowed by the mystery of Quaking-Asp Cabin. She had never known the secret of her father's deadness to her worship. He divined now, with terror gathering in a heart which had harbored only hate, that his insane passion for revenge had struck the child of the mother down.

All at once he saw Starke, a fine upstanding lad who adored Hillie, as the one to whom his starved heart had gone. And the Apache, stony-faced and sloe-eyed over her grave, buried his heart there, and left the homestead without farewell to the couple who had raised him. Richard never saw him again.

Richard was left alone with Blue. And hate, the fierce consumer, turned to ashes. It died without a flicker. Perhaps for long it had been unconsciously cooling. But the habit of silence abided with him. At the moment of death he could forgive Blue and Len. And he had strange inward tremors and loosenings as if the knotted cords of life had been untied. His hate, his passion might have kept him alive indefinitely. But these had perished and he saw himself as hideous of soul as he was deformed in body. If he relinquished this hold on life he would not last long.

When Matt came up again that spring Richard took him out to Hillie's grave, which was near the babbling brook, out of sight of the cabin. The Mormon did not hide his grief.

"Gone—that lovely child—without love or God." he exclaimed at length. "Dick, you failed in fatherhood . . . And Blue will be next to go."

"Friend, if I had it to live over . . . but no matter. I am a broken vessel . . . Do you ever see my brother?"

"Only seldom. But I can find him if you . . . "

"Fetch him, Matt. Then your loyal service to me will be ended. It bears this fruit. I shall ask you to pray to your God, as you prayed over me ten years ago, for mercy in the beyond."

Richard's decision seemed a letting go of the terrible force that had sustained him. If he let go utterly he knew that would be the end. He bade the Mormon depart and make haste on his errand.

That night, when the early twilight of autumn darkened the park, Richard looked out of the door. There were deer grazing with the cows. Frost breathed down from the heights. The moan of the pines, eternal it seemed to him, spoke of the long years, the travail, the end, the ways of the inscrutable. It was good that this lovely park and Quaking-Asp Cabin should go back to the wild. He would invest them with the shadow that had hovered over him, and which would deny this place to an abiding love of men.

Richard turned away from the door. Blue had just put a light upon the table, which was her mute signal that his supper was ready. But he approached his old armchair and sank into it.

"Blue." How strange—how hollow—mocking—the sound of that name on his lips—the first time in ten years. "I shall not eat tonight. . . .Come here."

She fell upon her knees beside him, and her hands like steel, clutched at his one arm.

"I have sent Matt to fetch Len."

"Oh, my God!" and the strength to go on seemed shaken out of her. White as it would ever be, her face dropped to his shoulder.

"I forgive you, Blue—and him. I should have forgiven long ago. But jealousy and hate have the power of hell . . . I might not last till he comes. For I have let go—and the fire that heated my heart is growing cold. . . . Tell him what I say . . . And this I leave you—not my wish, but my due—that you go away from Quaking-Asp forever. My doom has fallen upon it . . . See that bloody hand there on the chimney stone? By that Len marked this cabin—and I have fostered the shadow. It would blight any lives here—much more yours and Len's—who still have your great battle. If he has repented, as you have, my Blue, then there surely will be . . . But if he has sunk low—lift him up. He had a terrible strength of love for you. . . . There is money left that I hoarded—enough for you to go far away—as we all did once before—and begin life over again."

All day Richard had sat in his chair as if holding on to a taut and stretching cord, waiting for the clip-clap of hoofs. Blue flitted to and fro in the calm—silent, hovering back of him, peering out the door. In the silence he could hear her heart beat. But he could not even feel his own. Dusk stole in at the door and with it a cool sweet tang of the pines and the smell of burning leaves. That dusk darkened the room, accentuating the flickering sparks of the hearth. Or was it the creeping shadow that had darkened his mind? The old phantasms trooped back, detached, illusive. And on the moment when Blue's poignant cry rang out and the beat of hoofs pierced Richard's ear, a darkness came before his eyes to obliterate the mark of a spread hand on the chimney stone. And he thought it presaged the mantle of time—the generous years—the alchemy that had worked in him—the thing which lifted his failing heart to piercing gladness at the sound of the hoofbeats coming—faintly—fainter—lost.

LOST IN THE NEVER NEVER

In this fragment discovered after Zane Grey's death, the great writer known for his thrilling tales of life on the American plains, showed a different location: the wild Australian outback. It was a dangerous, primitive land, plagued by heat, drought, sandstorms, and savage aborigines.

Into this perilous territory came two American cowboys, Red Krehl and Sterl Hazelton. Sterl had left the United States after losing his girl had soured him on life, and wherever Sterl went his old pard Red was sure to follow.

Together they joined a cattle drive led by Stanley Dann and his partner Slyter—a drive that most men would never have considered possible. Unfamiliar with Australian cattle and terrain, Red and Sterl didn't realize what they were in for—and the last things they expected were treachery from Dann's own brother and the pleasant company of their bosses' daughters.

They came at length into a stranger, blacker, wilder country.

The dense growth of bush denoted a river—a river somewhere beyond the dark fringe of giant ash trees and bloodwoods and enormous trees with multiple trunks grotesque and gnarled. They camped where a huge wide-spreading banyan afforded a thick green canopy for the whole caravan. A boiling spring of sweet water ran away from the bank of bushland, forming a little stream that meandered away toward a pale lake, black and white with waterfowl. Kookaburras flew under the trees, perched on branches to watch the intruders, but they were silent. And that strange feature alone affected the morbid trekkers. The sun slanted in what appeared to be the wrong way and all was strange and different, even though all was as homelike and familiar as old Texas with its sunny prairies.

Never had Red thought that saddle and horseflesh would seem strange to him, but there it was again—the blending of the strange and the familiar. His mount was a tall animal with the lines of thoroughbred ancestry in his noble head, wide between the eyes and kindly in expression, the strong chest and deep barrel betokened an ability to travel long and fast. The saddle was lighter than he was used to and the irons more like the stirrups one would see on a race horse back home. It was a fine horse and good tack, but—again—all strangely different. He knew that he and Sterl could hold up their end in this cattle drive across the Australian desert, but there were times when he wished he were back in the dear old western plains.

"You reckon these critters will swim that

river?" Sterl said, breaking into Red's nostalgic daydreams. "I'd shore hate to see 'em bunch up and mill half way across. Or just whut *dew* these Australian cattle do when they hit water?"

"Old pard," said Red, "in a place where they've got animals the size of a deer that hop like jack rabbits, bears that will only live in eucalyptus trees and hev pouches like 'possums, where the sun slants the wrong way and even the stars are out of kilter, pard, I reckon I jest can't call the turn. These here cattle are more cold blooded than our long horns and range bred critters at home. Mebbe they'll be easier to handle. But if they get in a tight, can they fend for themselves like long horns? If I had my druthers I'd look for a better ford. Pard, I jest don't know."

Dann thrust out his chin like a snapping turtle at the sound of these opinions.

"Red Krehl, you said you wanted to see drovers at work and to help us drive a mob of cattle. Now you offer objections."

"Eric," said Red, "what I'm backin' off from is swimmin' a bunch of stock into a river like this. Why can't we scout around for a better crossing, with a hard bottom, shallow water and flat banks? This way it's likely we'll lose the job, a lot of cattle, an' somebody's life shore as Gawd made little apples. Damn, you're a cattleman as big as all this heah outdoors. But a dry land drover."

But Eric Dann's abnormal and malignant obsession again protruded its hydra head.

"Krehl is afraid," he shouted, hoarsely. "Once and for all, I demand to be heard. No foreigner is going to upset my plans—to make me ridiculous."

"Brother," rejoined the leader, "I ask you once more—do you know what you're doing when you advise us to cross this river?"

"Yes, I know. I know too, that Krehl is afraid. Ask him yourself. I'll ask him. See here, cowboy, are you man enough to confess the truth—that you *are* afraid?"

Red Krehl gave the drover a long, uncomprehending gaze. Dann was indeed a new one for the Texan. Then he spoke: "Hell yes. I shore am afraid of this river, the crocs an' the abos. But I reckon I oughta be more afraid of you, Mr. Dann. Because you're a queer mixture of fool, liar an' crook."

Sterl restrained himself until this argument ended, then he addressed the leader.

"Dann, I want you to know—and to remember—that I strongly advise against the attempt to cross this river here."

"Sorry, Hazelton. But we cross."

But the river and the tide had something to say about that, and when they were right, as near as the drovers thought they could be, then the cattle had the last word. This mob had been extraordinarily docile and easily managed, as the cowboys knew cattle. Many of the calves and cows that had distinguishing marks or habits that brought them into the daily notice had become pets. Toward the end of that day, however, they manifested evidences of a contrary disposition. About midafternoon Friday reported that they stopped grazing and became uneasy. Slyter went out to observe for himself. Upon his return he announced: "For some reason or other, they dislike this place."

"Then, we may be in for a night of it. I wouldn't care to try to stop a rush in this bush."

"Might be smellum crocs," said Friday.

Flying foxes had appeared during the afternoon, great, wide-winged grotesque bats, swishing out of the bush over the cattle, and their number increased toward sunset.

"Shore, it's them dinged bats thet have the herd buffaloed, an' they're gonna get us, too," said Red Krehl.

Here was one camp where a fire did not flame brightly, cheerily. The wood burned as if it were wet, and the smoke was acrid. Night settled down black, with the stars obscured by the foliage on three sides.

Supper had been eaten and five drovers had ridden out on guard when all left in camp were startled by a weird, droning sound off in the bush, apparently across the river.

"Black fella corroboree. 'Im no good," said Friday, his long black arm aloft.

Suddenly—a trampling roar of hoofs. The cowboys were as quick to leap up as Larry and Rollie. Slyter came thudding from his wagon. Eric Dann lifted a pale and haggard face. "A rush!" cried Stanley Dann.

"Aw, I knowed it," said Red, grimly. "Come, Sterl. Let's rustle our hosses."

"Wait, you cowboys," ordered Dann. "Some of us must guard the camp. Larry, Roland. Call Benson and join the drovers out there."

Slyter made off with the hurrying drovers, shouting something about his horses. Friday, at the edge of the circle of light, turned to the others and yelled, "Tinkit mob run alonga here."

"My God," boomed Stanley Dann. "Stand ready all. If the mob comes this way, take to the trees."

The increasing roar, the quaking ground, held all those listeners fraught with suspense and panic for an endless moment.

"Stampede'll miss us," yelled Red Krehl. Then Friday stooped to make violent motions with his right arm, indicating that the herd was rushing in the direction of the river. Gunshots banged faintly above the din.

"All right. We're safe," yelled Sterl, and then felt himself sag under the release of tension. It had been a few moments of terrible uncertainty.

Then a crashing augmented the trampling roar. The stampede, now evidently pointed up the river, had run into the bush. The noise lasted for minutes before it began to lessen in volume.

"Providence saved us again," rang out Stanley Dann, in immense relief. "But this rush will be bad for the mob."

"Dog-gone bad for the drovers, too, I'd say," declared Red.

"You may well think so, but usually a mob does not rush long. I am hopeful."

"They might stampede into the river," interposed Sterl.

Eric Dann sat down again and bent his gaze upon the ruddy fire embers. It was necessary to sit close to the heat and smoke to be even reasonably safe from mosquitoes. Eric Dann, however, sat back in the shadow. Not improbably he had too much on his mind to feel bites. Presently Slyter returned to camp.

"Horses all right," he was saying to Dann as they approached the fire. "The rush was bad. But half the mob were not affected."

"That was strange. Usually, cattle follow the leaders, like sheep. Uncanny sort of place."

"Righto. I jolly well wish we were out of it. Hello, Mum. You and Les should be in bed."

"I see ourselves with the mob threatening to run us down, and Stanley calling us to climb trees," retorted his good wife. "But we'll go now."

"Beryl, that would be a good idea for you," said her father.

"I'm afraid to go to bed,' replied the girl, petulantly.

"Me too," added Leslie. "These sneaky, furry bats give me the creeps. I just found one in our wagon. Ugh."

"Well, as long as Sterl and Red have to sit up, I suppose it's all right for you girls. But it's not a very cheerful place for courting."

Beryl let out a scornful little laugh. "Courting. Whom on earth with?"

"Sometime back it was royalty condescending. Now it's how the mighty have fallen," returned Mrs. Slyter, subtly, and left them.

"Leslie, whatever did your mother mean by that cryptic speech?" asked Beryl, annoyed.

"Oh, Mum's got softening of the brain," returned Leslie, and she dropped down on the log very close to Sterl. Red, who sat across the fire from them, looked up at Beryl, who was standing.

"Say, all you women have softenin' of the

brain," he drawled.

"Yeah?" queried Leslie.

"Is that so, Mr. Krehl?" added Beryl.

"Yes, it's so. Take that crack of Leslie's mother, for instance. Les's Ma an' you girls air of one mind, I reckon. The idee is to collar a man, any man temporarily, till you meet up with one you aim to corral for keeps."

"That is true, Red. Disgustingly true," admitted Beryl, suddenly frank and earnest. "But Les and I are not to blame for being born women."

"I reckon not, Beryl," returned Red, conciliated by her sincerity.

"Go on, Red. You *were* going to say something," went on Beryl.

"I was," rejoined the cowboy. "It seemed to me kind of far-fetched an' silly—thet sentimental yearnin' of yores, if it was thet. Heah we air lost in this Gawd-foresaken land. Aw, I know Eric there swears we ain't lost, but thet doesn't fool me. An' this hole is as spooky an' nasty a place as I ever camped. It's more. It's a darned dangerous one. We jest escaped somethin' tough. An' thet's why I jest wondered at you womenfolks, feelin' thet soft, sweet mushy sentiment in the face of hell."

"Red Krehl, that's the wonder of it—that we *can* feel and need such things at such a time," returned Beryl, eloquently. "I left such things behind, to come with my father. I could have gone to live in Sydney. But I came with Dad. And you've seen something of what I've suffered. This hard experience has not wholly destroyed my sensitiveness, my former habits. I can see why Sterl thinks we're going bush. I can see that we'll turn into abos, if we're stuck here forever. But just now, I've a dual nature. By day I'm courageous, by night I'm cowardly. I can't sleep. I'm afraid of noises. I lie with the cold chills creeping over me. I can't forget what—what has already happened to me. Red Krehl, you said you wonder at me. But I say it's a wonder you cannot see how I'd welcome any kindness, any attention, any affection, to keep me from thinking."

It was a long speech, though quickly spoken, one that Sterl took to his heart in shame and self reproach. He was intensely curious to see how Red would take it, and somehow he had faith in the cowboy's greatness of soul.

"Come heah, girl," said Red, gently, and held out his hand. Beryl stepped to him and leaned, as if compelled. He drew her to a place beside him on the narrow pack, and he put his arm around her to draw her close. "I'm sorry I made all them hard cracks about this place. Only I'm glad, 'cause I understand you better. But Beryl, I reckon you can't figger me out. When all was goin' fine back on this trek you gave me some pretty bad times. So, even if I wanted to be sweet an' soft about you, which I shore don't after the way you treated me, I couldn't be on account of what this damn trek has done to me. I've saved yore life a coupla times, an I reckon I'll have to do thet a heap more. If I wasn't a hard-ridin', hard-shootin' cowboy, a killer, grim an' mean, I couldn't do thet much for you. Thet ought to make you see me clear."

"Oh, Red," said Beryl, poignantly, "I don't want you any different."

The thud of hoofs disrupted this scene, and

Larry rode up. Friday came running to throw brush upon the blaze.

"Larry, you're all bloody," exclaimed Sterl.

"No. I just ran—into a snag," panted the drover. "Let me—fetch water and linen."

Dann arrived to bend over Larry. "Bad scalp cut. Girls, fetch water and linen. Larry, are you all right?"

"Yes sir—except played out."

"Where are the other drovers?"

"Back with what was left of the mob. That rush got—away, sir."

"How many?"

"Benson said one-third of the mob. They rushed into the bush. They were a crazy lot of cattle. They crashed through the bush—some into the river. So we yelled to come together—then rode back. That mob will work out of the bush by morning."

Meanwhile Dann had unwound the scarf from Larry's head and begun to dress the wound. Slyter told the girls to go to bed, and this time they obeyed. Red was sent off to take Larry's place with the drovers and Sterl ordered to stay in camp.

When toward dawn Red and Rollie came in, relieved by two of Dann's drovers, Sterl lay down beside Red. The sun was up when Friday called them.

"Where black fella, Friday?"

"Alonga dere. No good. Hidum about. Watchum white man."

"Sterl, these abos up heah 'pear to be a different breed. All same as Comanche Injuns," said Red.

They found the drovers straggling in. Benson reported two-thirds of the mob intact. Their ragged garb, scratched hands, bruised faces gave evidence of their strenuous effort to head that rush.

"We stopped it, five miles west," reported Bligh, wearily. "They're out in the open, not many on their feet. Dehorned, crippled, snagged—a sorry mess."

Friday appeared, carrying a kangaroo that he had speared.

"Plenty roo," he said. "Ribber full up. Plenty croc."

"Friday, see any blacks?" asked Sterl.

"Black fella imm alonga bush. Bimeby."

"Men, eat and drink all you can hold," said Stanley Dann. "We'll leave those cattle that started the rush last night until the last. If they scatter, we'll abandon them. Our mob has been too large. We'll break camp now. Move all the wagons and horses to the open break in the bush below. Then drive the main mob closer. Two guards on and off for two hours. We'll ford the river with the wagons, divide our party and camp on both sides until the last job, which will be to drove the mob across."

It was a bold and masterly plan, Sterl conceded. The execution would be an heroic job. They mounted and rode away.

The river. The drovers, even their leader, had only to go within sight of that reed-bordered, mud-sloped, yellow swirling tide to be confronted by seeming impossibilities.

"Friday, where are the crocodiles?" boomed Dann.

"Alonga dere," replied the black, his spear indicating the river and the margins of reeds.

"Slyter, do they hide in the grass?"

"Yes, indeed. These big crocs live on animals. This water is brackish. Kangaroos, wild cattle, brumbies would drink it. I've been told how the crocs lie in wait and with one lash of their tails knock a large animal or an aborigine into the water."

"They may not be plentiful. But all of you use your eyes. Have your guns ready. Slyter, you will drive your wagon in first. Send a drover ahead to test the bottom. Make haste, while the tide is in."

They all watched Heald wade his sturdy horse into the river. After perhaps a hundred steps, he returned to say: "Mud bottom. Soft. But not quicksand. If you keep your horse moving you can make it."

"What will a heavy wagon do?" queried Slyter, dubiously.

"It'll stick, but not sink," declared Dann. "We have heavy ropes and strong horses. We can pull out." In a moment more, Slyter, accompanied by Dann and six drovers, had driven his big teams into the river.

Slyter had not got quite so far out as Heald had waded when the wheels stuck. Two drovers leaped out of their saddles to unhitch the teams. Bligh and Hood dragged the teams out. Rollie, with a bag in front of him and a cracking stockwhip in hand, kept abreast of the teams. Soon they were swimming. Four drovers followed carrying packs. Slyter stood up in his wagon, rifle in hand, watching vigilantly.

"Crocs over dere all alonga," cried Friday, pointing.

Sterl saw the reeds shake and part. "Grab your rifle, Red," he shouted.

Suddenly on the opposite bank there was a loud rush in the reeds, then a zoom, as a huge reptile leaped off the bank and slid upon the narrow strip of mud. But it was not quick enough to escape Red's shot.

Sterl heard the bullet thud, and then the huge reptile flopped up and flashed into convulsions. Sterl let out a yell as he drew a bead upon it and pulled the trigger. The distance was nothing to a marksman. His bullet, too, found its mark.

Another. Four shots left that reptile rolling in the mud. Its back seemed broken.

"Dere, along dere," shrilled Friday, pointing below.

Slyter was shooting at another one, smaller and nimbler. But there was another rush and zoom as a big one catapulted off the bank to meet a hail of lead. Crippled and slow, he crawled into the river.

Stanley Dann's horse appeared, wading out. The drovers dragged and yelled at the teams, while Rollie cracked his long whip from behind. They got across at last and climbed the bank to deposit the packs and find a place to land the wagon. Then they piled into the river—pell-mell, keeping close together, some of them with drawn guns held high.

Slyter yelled, "Make all the commotion possible."

They crossed in short order and turned back in haste and crossed again. Suddenly Friday screeched out something aboriginal. Then Slyter roared unintelligibly, and began to pump lead into the water. A thumping splash followed, then a vicious churning of the surface, yellow and red mixing.

"I got him," shouted Slyter, peering down. "Right on top of me. Longer than the wagon. Never saw him till he came up."

When the drovers arrived at the wagon again, Stanley Dann called out lustily: "Boys, that was splendid work. I heard your big bullets hit. It's not so bad having Yankee gunmen with us."

During nine more trips, while Slyter, Larry and the black kept vigil from several points, nothing untoward happened. Dann, with three of the drovers, then remained on the far side with the teams backed out into the shallow water. The other three, dragging tackle and ropes, swam their horses back to make fast to the wagon.

Bligh slid off his horse, and waist-deep groped about with his feet to find the wagon tongue. To watch him thus exposed made the cold sweat ooze out all over Sterl. Bligh found it, and went clear under to lift it up. In a moment more the two teams sagged down and dug in; the drovers in front of the wagon laid hold of the thick rope. Slyter lifted his arms on high, swung his rifle, and added his yell to that of the others. A moment of strain and splash—then the empty wagon lurched, moved, half floated. Slyter stood up on the driver's seat, balancing himself, still peering into the water for crocodiles. The two teams and the six single horses did not slow up until the wheels touched bottom. In a very few moments the wagon was safely up on the bank. Despite the crocodiles, the achievement augured well for the success of the operation.

All this time the tide was slowly going out. The channel split wide, exposing bare stretches of mud. Sterl observed that a big crocodile which he had thought surely killed had disappeared from the bank opposite. The one Slyter had shot lay on its back, claw-like feet above the shallow water.

Some of Dann's party cut poles and brush to lay lengthwise on the mud over the plowed up tracks of wheels and horses. Bill set about erecting a canvas shelter to work under. Sterl, Red and Friday hurried at camp tasks the crossing had halted. Presently Slyter and Dann's drovers, all except Roland, who had been left on the far side of the river, arrived muddy and wet, noisy and triumphant, back in camp.

"Volunteer wanted to drive the small dray," called the leader.

They all wanted that job. Dann chose Benson, the eldest. Six men cut brushy trees while two riders snaked these down to the river. Dann and Slyter built the corduroy road. Eric Dann lent a hand, like one in a trance. Friday pointed to aborigine smoke signals far back in the bush, and shook his shaggy head.

Many energetic hands made short work of the road on the camp side of the river. It was significant that Slyter covered his dead crocodile with brush. Then Benson drove the one-team dray off the bank. The brush road upheld both horses and wheels as long as they moved. But it stuck in the channel, and, before it crossed, the drovers had to unload it and carry its contents to the far bank. By this time the afternoon was far spent, and Bill had supper ready. Benson volunteered to pack supper across to Roland and Bligh, left on guard, and remain over there with them.

The drovers, bedraggled, slimy from the river mud, ate like wolves, but were too tired to talk. Sterl and Red went out on duty with the mob.

Again the night was silent, except for the bark of dingoes and the silken swish of flying foxes. But the mob appeared to be free from the fears of the night before. Sterl and Red kept together, and after a few hours, one of them watched while the other slept. But Sterl, in his wakeful intervals, could not rid himself of misgivings. His mind conjured up fateful events for which there seemed no reason.

At last the dawn came, from gray to daylight, and then a ruddiness in the east. He awakened Red from his hard bed on the grass. They rounded up the remuda, and changed their mounts for King and Duke.

"Red, it's dirty business to risk Leslie's horses in that river," said Sterl, as they rode campward.

"Wal, I was thinkin' the same. We won't do it, 'cept to cross them. We'll fork two of these draft hosses. But, holy mackeli, they cain't keep one of them crocs away. I swear, pard, I never had my gizzard freeze like it does at thet thought."

"Nerve and luck, Red."

"Them drovers shore had it yestiddy."

Breakfast was over at sunrise. Friday approached the fire to get his fare.

"Crocs alonga eberywhere," he announced.

That silenced the trekkers like a clap of thunder. Slyter, the cowboys, and the drovers followed the striding Dann out to view the stream. A dead steer floated by in mid-channel, gripped by several crocodiles. Downstream a cow or steer had stranded in the shallow water. Around it ugly snouts and notched tails showed above the muddy water. Upstream on the far side a third cow, stuck in the mud, was surrounded by the reptiles.

Larry explained, "Night before last a number of cattle rushed into the river. We heard them bawling and plunging."

Slyter said, "Blood scent in the river will have every croc for miles down upon us."

"It may not be so bad as it looks," replied the leader with his usual optimism. "Let's cross Bill's dray at once. Tell Bill to keep out food and tea for today and tomorrow. One of you to put tucker on the dray for the boys across there. A kettle of hot tea. Who'll drive Bill's dray?"

Red Krehl elected himself for that job. But Dann preferred to have the cowboy on shore, rifle in hand, and selected Heald. He drove in until the water came almost to the platform of the wagon. Then the procedure of the day before was carried out with even more celerity. It struck Sterl that in their hurry the drovers were forgetting about the crocodiles, which might have been just as well. This big job done the drovers took time out for a cup of tea. That inevitable rite amused Sterl.

"Ormiston's wagon next," shouted Stanley Dann. "That duty falls to Eric."

The drovers hitched two teams to this wagon, while others, at the leader's order, unpacked half of its contents. Flour in special burlap sacks and other food supplies came to light.

At the take-off the leading team balked, and upon being urged and whipped they plunged, and Eric laid on the stockwhip. No doubt a scent of the dead crocodiles came to them. Stanley Dann boomed orders that Eric did not hear or could not obey. About a hundred steps out was as far as either of the other vehicles had been driven. But Eric drove until the teams balked, with the leaders submerged to their shoulders. This was extremely bad, because it was evident that they were sinking in the mud. Half a dozen drovers urged plunging horses to the rescue.

At that critical moment Friday let out a wild yell. Sterl saw a dead steer, surrounded by crocodiles, drifting down upon the teams.

"Back, Heald. Back, Hood," shouted Sterl, at the top of his lungs. "Crocs."

Snorting, lunging, the horses wheeled and sent mountains of water flying. They reached the shore just as the dead steer drifted upon the teams and lodged. Stanley Dann was yelling for his brother to climb back over the wagon and leap for his life. Eric might have heard, but his gaze was glued to the melee under him.

The dead steer drifted in between the two teams to lodge against the wagon tongue. And the great reptiles attacked the horses. The snap of huge jaws, the crack of teeth, could be heard amid the roar of water and the clamor of the drovers.

Eric pulled his gun and shot. As you might expect, he hit the horses instead of the crocodiles. The left front horse reared high with a crocodile hanging to its nose. Sterl sent a bullet into its head, but it did not let go. It pulled the horse under. The right front horse was in the clutches of two crocodiles. The open jaws of one stuck beyond the neck of the horse. Krehl's rifle cracked. Sterl shot to kill a horse if he missed a crocodile. The second team had been attacked by a half dozen of the leviathans.

And at that awful moment for Eric Dann, horses and wagon were pulled into deep water. The wagon sank above its bed and floated. Eric leaped to the driver's seat and held on. As he turned to those on shore his visage appeared scarcely human. The wagon drifted down the river.

"Fellers, fork yore hosses," yelled Red. Leaping on Duke, his rifle aloft, he raced into the bush downstream. Sterl was quick to follow, and he heard the thud and crash of the drovers at his heels. When he broke out into the clear, a low bank afforded access to the river, which made a bend there. He came out at the edge of the mud. Red had Duke wading out. The wagon had lodged in shallow water. A horrible fight was going on there. Beyond it several other crocodiles were tearing at a horse that had been cut adrift. Eric Dann still clung to the driver's seat.

Stanley Dann and his followers arrived. For

once, the leader's booming voice was silent at a crisis.

Red threw aside his rifle. He held his revolver in his left hand and his lariat in his right. At that moment, a lean, black-jawed crocodile stuck his snout and shoulders out of the water, and, reaching over the wagonbed, snapped at Eric. He missed by more than two feet.

The horses had ceased to struggle. What with the tugging and floundering of the crocodiles the wagon appeared about to tilt over. It would all be over with Eric Dann if the reptiles did not tear the horses free.

Red sent his grand horse plunging into the water. Duke's ears stood up, his piercing snorts made the other horses neigh wildly. Red was taking a chance that the crocodiles would be too busy to see him. When Duke was up to his flanks and the curdled, foamy maelstrom scarcely a lasso's length distant, Red yelled piercingly: "Stand up, Eric."

The man heard, and tried to obey. But he must have been paralyzed with horror.

"Stick out yore laig—yore arm," shrieked Red, in a fury, and he shot the outside crocodile, sliding into view.

But Eric was beyond helping himself. Again that ugly brute lunged out and up, his corrugated jaws wide, and as they snapped they missed by only a few inches.

Then the lasso shot out, and the noose cracked over Eric's head and shoulders. Red whirled the big horse and spurred him shoreward. Eric was jerked off the wagon, over the very backs of the threshing crocodiles. Red dragged him free, through the shallow water, up on the mud. He leaped off, to run and loosen the noose. Eric's head had been dragged through the mud. Stanley and drovers lifted the half-dead man, and carried him ashore. Sterl sat on his horse with his throat constricted. He had not cared much about Eric Dann, but the mad risk that intrepid cowboy had run....

"He ain't—hurt none," Red panted, coiling the muddy rope. "I was afraid—I'd get the noose—'round his neck. But it was a damn narrow shave. Pard, that's one hoss—in a million. By Gawd, I was scared he—wouldn't do it. But he did—he did."

They laid Eric Dann on the bank to let him recover. Sterl dismounted, and every time a head or a body lunged up he met it with a bullet. But the angle was bad. Most of the bullets glanced singingly across the river. One by one the horses were torn loose from the traces, and dragged away, until they disappeared under the deep water.

The heavy wagon had remained upright, with the back end and wheels submerged. The tide was falling.

"Miraculous, any way you look at it," exclaimed Stanley Dann. "Red Krehl, as if my debt to you had not been great enough."

"Hell, boss. We've all been around yestiddy an' today, when things came off," drawled the cowboy.

At low tide Ormiston's wagon was hauled out

and back to camp. The girls clamored for the story. Red laughed at them, but Sterl told it, not wholly without elaboration. He wanted to see Beryl Dann's eyes betray her quick and profound emotions.

"For my uncle. Red—when he hated you."

"Beryl, all in the day's ride," drawled Red. "Now if you was only like Duke."

"Red, I am not a horse, I am a woman," she rejoined with no response to his humor.

"Shore, I know thet. I mean a hoss, if he's great like Duke an' cottons to a feller, why he'll do anythin' for you." Red also had turned serious. "Beryl, I'd die for him, an' shore he'd die for me."

"I'd like you to feel that way for me, Red Krehl," she returned vibrantly. "I would die for you."

"Wal, yore wants, like yore eyes an' yore heart, air too big for you, Beryl."

Leslie let go of Duke's neck to face Red.

"Red, I give Duke to you. And you can return Jester to me," she said.

"Wal dog-gone it, Les, you hit me below the belt."

"It'll make me happy. And Beryl too."

Stanley Dann broke in upon them with his booming order; "Cut more poles. We'll relay the road and cross my wagon before this day is done."

While his drovers worked like beavers, he had Beryl's bed and baggage unloaded. Stanley drove his big wagon across. Friday sighted crocodiles, but none came near. Load and wagon were crossed in record time, after which six drovers carried

Beryl's belongings across in two trips.

The sun set red and evil. The trekkers ate, and tried to be oblivious to the abo signals, the uncanny bats, the howls of the dingoes and the unseen menace that hovered over this somber camp. Stanley Dann roused them all in the gray of dawn. It was wet and chill. Dingoes bayed dismally in the bush. The cowboys found two of Dann's drovers mustering horses for the day. The cowboys bridled Duke, King and Lady Jane, and drove the rest of Leslie's horses into camp. Stanley Dann's hearty voice, his spirit, the drab gray dawn lighting ruddily, the hot breakfast—all seemed to work against the gripping, somber spell.

"Men, this is our important day," boomed the leader. "Roland's wagon first. Unload all the heavy articles. Pack these bags of dried fruit Ormiston had—unknown to me. Slyter, will you drive Roland's wagon?"

"Yes," replied Slyter. "Mum, you ride with me."

"With Beryl and Leslie that will be a load," said Dann.

"Dad, I won't cross in the wagon," spoke up his daughter decidedly.

Leslie interposed to say, "I'm riding Lady Jane."

The leader gazed at these pioneer daughters with great luminous eyes, and made no further comment. He hurried the unpacking, and the hitching of two big draft horses to Roland's wagon. The sun came up gloriously bright. When Slyter mounted the high wagon seat, shouts from across the river told him that the drovers over there were ready. Roland straddled one of the lead horses of the teams. The tide was on the make, wanting a foot in height and a dozen yards up the mud bank to fill the river bed.

"Friday. Everybody watch the river for crocs," ordered the leader.

Leslie sat her horse, pale and resolute. She knew the peril. At this juncture Beryl emerged from the tent, slim in her rider's garb. She carried a small black bag.

"Red, will you carry me across?" she asked, simply. Her darkly dilated eyes betrayed her terror.

"Shore, Beryl, but why for?" drawled the cowboy.

"I'd feel safer—and—and—"

"Wal, dog-gone. There. Put yore foot on my stirrup. Up you come. No, I cain't hold you that way, Beryl. You've gotta fork Duke. Slip down in front of me. Sterl, how about slopin'?"

"Friday grins good-o," replied Sterl, grimly. "Les, keep above me close. Larry, keep upstream from Red. Idea is to move pronto."

They plunged in, passed Slyter's teams and the drovers, reached the deeper water, breasted the channel.

"Fellers, get ready for gunplay," shouted the hawk-eyed Red. "Shet yore eyes, Beryl."

Across the river from the reedy bank above Roland's position came a crackling rush, a waving of reeds, then a zoom, as a big crocodile took to the water. The guns of Roland's group banged; mud splattered all around the reptile.

Farther upstream, muddy-backed crocodiles, as huge as logs, piled into the river. The drovers were clamoring in fright and excitement. Slyter had driven his teams in up to their flanks. One drover was unfastening the traces, while two others were ready to drag the teams into the channel. Sterl spared only a glance for them. Roland and his men came pounding through the shallow water. Halfway across—two-thirds. Bligh's horse was lunging into the channel above Larry, carrying the tackle and rope for the wagon.

Suddenly, almost in line with them, an openjawed, yellow-fanged monster spread the reeds, and zoomed off the bank. Red, Sterl, Larry, Roland, were shooting. But the crocodile came on, got over his depth, and disappeared.

"Watch for the wake," called Red. "Thet feller is mean. Heah he comes. See them little knobs. That's his haid."

Sterl espied them. He regretted having left his rifle in the wagon.

"Drop behind me, Leslie," he called. "Don't weaken. We'll get by him."

Sterl did not fire because he did not want to drive the brute under water again. Evidently Red had the same thought. He headed Duke quarterly away from the long ripple, and leaned far forward, gun extended. His left arm held the drooping girl. At the right instant he spurred Duke. Just then Duke struck bottom, and lunged. The crocodile was less than six feet distant when Red turned his gun loose. The bullets splashed and thudded, but they did not glance. With a tremendous swirl the reptile lurched partly out of the water, a ghastly spectacle. Sterl sent two leaden slugs into it. Falling back, the monster began to roll over and over, his ten-foot tail beating the water into foam.

Red waded Duke past the teams and waiting drovers, out onto the bank. The drovers cheered. Sterl, with Leslie behind him, followed Red up to the new camp. Red slid off and laid his gun on the grass. Beryl swayed, her eyes tight shut.

"Beryl, come out of it," shouted Red. Her arms fell weakly.

"I won't—faint. I won't," she cried with passion still left in her weak voice.

"Who said you would?" drawled Red, as he helped her off.

Leslie dismounted and came to Beryl. They clung together—a gesture more eloquent than any words.

"Come, pard. Let's slope out there," called Red.

When they rode out on the mud flat again Sterl was amazed to see Friday dragging what evidently was the monster crocodile into shallow water. A long spear sticking in the reptile spoke for itself. A splashing melee distracted Sterl. The two teams were straining on the ropes, plowing through the mud. Between them and the wagon the drovers were yelling and hauling. Sterl observed that this wagon, the one in which he had calked the seams, floated almost flat. Mrs. Slyter stood behind her husband, hanging on to the seat while he made ready for the waiting teams. Once the wagon was in shallow water they unfastened the ropes and tackles, hitched the two teams and gave Slyter the word to drive out.

Sterl and Red followed the muddy procession up the bank.

Friday said to Sterl and Slyter, "Tinkit more better boss wait alonga sun. Crocs bad."

"We can't stop Dann now," Slyter said, grimly. "Come, all who're going back."

"Wal, if you ask me we oughta load our guns," drawled Red.

Five drovers crossed the river with Sterl and Red. Dann met them like a general greeting a victorious army.

"We've time to drove Slyter's horses across and carry these loose supplies," he said. "Tomorrow we will muster the cattle that rushed and drove the mob."

When next morning the drovers had the big herd lengthened out to perhaps half a mile, at a signal from Dann they opened fire with their guns and charged. The fifty-yard-wide belt of cattle headed for the river and piled over the low bank. Across the river crocodiles basked in the sun, their odor thick on the air. The leading cattle took fright and balked. Then it was too late. The pushing, bawling lines behind forced them on. Some of them were bogged, to be trampled under. But almost miraculously the mob were driven into the mud before they could attempt a rush back.

The point of least resistance lay to the fore. The leaders had to gravitate that way. From the opposite bank crocodiles slid down and shot across the mud into the shallow water. Released from a wall in front, the mass behind piled frantically into the river. As if by a miracle, thousands of horned heads breasted the channel. In several spots swirling, churning battles ensued, almost at once to be overridden by swimming cattle. As the front line struck bottom the stench of the crocodiles and their furious attack precipitated a rush that was obscured in flying spray.

"Come on, pard," yelled Red, from below. "We wanta be close behind that stampede or the crocs will get us."

All the other drovers were in the mud, some at the heels of the mob, others shooting crippled and smashed cattle. The horse herd, driven in the wake of the mob, excited by the roar, made frantic efforts to get ahead. When they found bottom again, and plunged on into shallow water, Sterl looked up.

A sea of bobbing backs sloped up to a fringe of bobbing horns. The long belt of cattle was moving with amazing speed. Sterl gazed back. More cattle dotted the river. Squirming crocodiles attested to the trampling they had received. Only one horse was down, and it appeared to be struggling to rise.

"Laig broke," yelled Red, close to Sterl's ear. "Saddled too. By Gawd, pard, that's Eric Dann's hoss. An' if he ain't lyin' there on the mud, my eyes air pore."

Stanley Dann and two others appeared riding at

a gallop. The leader was pointing at the fallen horse and rider. Sterl and Red had already headed in his direction.

"Look—a croc slipping off into deep water," yelled Sterl.

Stanley Dann reached the prostrate man and horse ahead of Bligh and Heald. Sterl and Red got there as the drovers were dismounting, to sink ankle-deep in the mud.

"It's Eric," boomed the leader, as he leaned over. "Dead—or—no. He's still alive."

"Horses front legs broken," reported Bligh, tensely.

"Shoot it. And help me—two of you."

They lifted him across Bligh's saddle. How limp he hung. What a slimy, broken wreck of a man.

"Hazelton, you and Krehl and Heald follow the mob," ordered the leader, harshly. "That rush will end soon."

From the height of the bank Sterl looked over bushland and green downs which led to higher and denser bush. In the foreground, the mob of cattle had halted.

"All the stampede is out of them," said Red.

"Crocodile stampede. New one on us, Red," rejoined Sterl.

"Cost Dann and Slyter plenty. Hundreds of cattle down, daid an' dyin'. Sterl, about Dann's drovers—after this last shuffle, what's the deal gonna be?"

"You mean if Eric Dann holds up the trek?"

"I shore mean that little thing."

"Damn serious, pard."

"Serious? If Bligh an' Hood an' the others stick it out. I'd say it'll be a damn sight more than any Americans would do. 'Cept a couple of dumb-haid, lovesick suckers like us."

When the cowboys arrived, the cattle had begun to lie down, too exhausted even to bawl. The horses had scattered off to the left toward camp. Sterl and Red helped muster them and drove them within sight of the wagons.

"What held up Stanley Dann?" inquired Bligh, as the drovers collected again. Bligh was a young man, under thirty, gray-eyed and still-faced, a man on whom the other drovers leaned.

"Eric injured. Legs broken I think," replied Sterl.

Bligh exchanged apprehensive glances with his intimates. He turned back to Sterl: "If the boss's brother is unable to travel, it'll precipitate a most serious situation."

"We appreciate that. Let's hope it's not so bad he cannot be moved in a wagon."

"Yes. You hope so, but you don't believe it." said Bligh, brusquely.

"Righto."

"Hazelton, we all think you and Krehl are wonderful drovers, and what is more, right good cobbers," said Bligh, feelingly.

"Thanks, Bligh," returned Sterl, heartily. "Red and I sure return the compliment."

"For us this trek seems to have run into a forlorn hope."

"Well, Bligh, I'm bound to agree with you. But it's not a lost cause yet."

The drover shook his shaggy head, and ran skinned, dirty fingers through his scant beard. "Friend, it's different with you cowboys, on account of the girls—if you'll excuse my saying so."

Neither Beryl nor Leslie put in an appearance at supper. Dann seemed for once an unapproachable figure. Slyter conversed in low tones with his wife, and once Sterl saw him throw up his hands in a singular gesture for him. Red stayed in the tent. The seven young drovers remained in a group at the other side of camp, where Bligh appeared to be haranguing them.

Suddenly Bligh, leading Derrick, Hod and Heald, rose and started toward Stanley Dann's shelter. Pale despite their tans, resolute despite their fear. It did not seem a coincidence that Beryl and Leslie appeared from nowhere; that Slyter came out, his hair ruffled, his gaze fixed; that Red emerged from his tent, his lean hawklike head poised; that Friday hove in sight, lending to the scene the stark reality of the aborigine.

Under Dann's shelter it was still light. Mrs. Slyter stood beside the stretcher where Eric Dann lay, his head and shoulders propped up on pillows, fully conscious and ghastly pale. His legs were covered with a blanket. Stanley Dann sat with bowed head. The drovers halted just outside of the shelter. Bligh took a further step.

"Mr. Dann, is it true Eric is injured?" burst out Bligh, as if forced.

Dann rose to his full height to stare at his visitors. He stalked out then like a man who faced death.

"Bligh, I grieve to inform you that he is," he said.

"We are—very sorry for him—and you," rejoined Bligh huskily.

"I'm sure of that, Bligh."

"Will it be possible to move him? In a wagon, you know, to carry on our trek?"

"No. Even with proper setting of the bones he may be a cripple for life. To move him now—over rough ground—would be inhuman."

"What do you intend to do?"

"Stay here until he is mended enough to travel."

"That would take weeks, sir. Perhaps more . . ."

"Yes. Weeks. There is no alternative."

Bligh made a gesture of inexpressible regret. He choked. He cleared his throat. "Mr. Dann, we—we feared this very thing . . . We talked it over. We can't—we won't—go on with this wild-goose trek. You started all right. Then Ormiston and your brother . . . No sense in crying over spilled milk. We've stuck to the breaking point. We four have decided to trek back home."

"Bligh — *you too?*" boomed the leader. Sterl saw him change as if he had shriveled up inside.

"Yes, me." rang out Bligh. "You ask too much of young men. We built our hopes on your promises. Hood has a wife and child. Derrick is sick of this . . . We are going home."

"Bligh, I have exacted too much of you all," returned Dann. "I'm sorry. If I had it do over again. . . . You are welcome to go, and God speed you. . . . Take two teams for Ormiston's wagon. It is half full of food supplies. Bill will give you a box of tea. And if you can muster the cattle that rushed up the river—you are welcome to them."

"Boss—that is big and fine—of you," returned Bligh, haltingly. "Honestly, sir. . . ."

"Don't thank me, Bligh. I am in your debt."

Eric Dann called piercingly from under the shelter. "Bligh, tell him—tell him."

"Tell me what?" boomed the leader, like an angry lion aroused. "Bligh, what have you to tell me?"

"Nothing, sir. Eric is out of his head."

"No I'm not," yelled Eric, and his attempt to push himself higher on the stretcher ended in a shriek of pain. But he did sit up, and Mrs. Slyter supported him.

"Eric, what could Bligh tell me?" queried Stanley Dann, hoarsely.

There ensued a silence that seemed insupportable to Sterl. Every moment added to the torment of coming terrible disclosures. Eric Dann must have been wrenched by physical pain and mental anguish to a point beyond resistance. "Stanley—we are lost," he groaned.

"Lost?" echoed the giant, blankly.

"Yes—yes. Lost," cried Eric wildly. "We've been lost all the way. I didn't know this bushland. I've never been on a trek through outback Queensland."

"Merciful heaven!" boomed the leader, his great arms going aloft. "Your plans? Your assurances? Your map?"

"Lies. All lies," wailed Eric Dann. "I never was inland—from the coast. I met Ormiston. He talked cattle. He inflamed me about a fabulous range in the Northern Territory—west of the Gulf. Gave me the map we've trekked by. I planned with him to persuade you to muster a great mob of cattle. . . . I didn't know that he was the bushranger Pell. That map is false. I couldn't confess—I couldn't—I kept on blindly. We're lost—Bligh knows that. Ormiston could not corrupt him. Yet he wouldn't betray me to you. We're lost—irretrievably lost. And I'm damned—to hell."

Stanley Dann expelled a great breath and sat down on a pack as if his legs had been chopped from under him.

"Lost? Yea, God has forsaken me," he whispered.

Bligh was the first to move after a stricken silence. "Mr. Dann, you've got to hear that I didn't know all Eric confessed."

"Bligh, that is easy to believe, thank heaven," said Stanley presently, his voice gaining timbre. "We'll thresh it all out right now. . . . Somebody light a fire to dispel this hateful gloom. Let me think a moment." And he paced somberly to and fro outside the shelter. Presently Stanley Dann faced them and the light, once more himself.

"Listen, all of you," he began, and again his voice had that wonderful deep roll. "I cannot desert my brother. Whoever does stay here with me must carry on with the trek when we are able to continue. I have exacted too much of you all. I grieve that I have been wrong, self-centered, dominating. Beryl, my daughter, will you stay?"

"Dad, I'll stay." There was no hesitation in Beryl's reply, and to Sterl she seemed at last of her father's blood and spirit. "Don't despair, Dad. We shall not all betray you."

A beautiful light warmed his grave visage as he turned to Leslie. "Child, you have been forced into womanhood. I doubt if your parents should influence your decision here."

"I would not go back to marry a royal duke," replied Leslie.

"Mrs. Slyter, your girl has indeed grown up on this trek," went on Dann. "But she will still need a mother. Will you stay?"

"Need you ask, Stanley? I don't believe whatever lies in store for us could be so bad as what we've lived through," rejoined the woman calmly.

"Slyter?"

"Stanley, I started the race and I'll make the good fight."

"Hazelton!" demanded Dann, without a trace of doubt. His exclamation was not a query.

"I am keen to go on," answered Sterl.

"Krehl."

The cowboy was lighting a cigarette, a little clumsily, because Beryl was clinging to his arm. He puffed a cloud of smoke which hid his face.

"Wal, boss," he drawled, "it's shore a great privilege you've given me. Jest a chance to know an' fight for a man."

Larry, Rollie, and Benson, almost in unison, hastened to align themselves under Red's banner.

Bill, the cook, stepped forward and unhesitatingly spoke: "Boss, I've had enough. I'm getting old. I'll go home with Bligh."

"Bingham, put it up to our black man Friday," said Dann.

Slyter spoke briefly in that jargon which the black understood.

Friday leaned on his long spear and regarded the speakers with his huge, unfathomable eyes. Then he swerved them to Sterl and Red, to Beryl, to Leslie, and tapped his broad black breast with a slender black hand: "Imm no fadder, no mudder, no brudder, no gin, no lubra," he said, in slow, laborious dignity. "Tinkit go bush along white fella cowboy pards."

At another time Sterl would have shouted his gladness, but here he only hugged the black man. And Red clapped him on the back.

Suddenly a heavy gunshot boomed hollowly under the shelter, paralyzing speech and action. The odor of burnt powder permeated the air. There followed a queer, faint tapping sound—a shuddering quiver of hand or foot of a man in his death throes. Sterl had heard that too often to be deceived. Stanley Dann broke out of his rigidity to wave a shaking hand.

"Go in—somebody—see," he whispered.

Benson and Bligh went slowly and hesitatingly under the shelter. Sterl saw them lean over Eric on the stretcher. They straightened up. Bligh drew a blanket up over the man's face. That pale blot vanished under the dark covering. The drovers stalked out. Bligh accosted the leader in hushed voice: "Prepare for a shock, sir."

Benson added gruffly: "He blew his brains out."

Red Krehl was the first to speak, as he drew Beryl away from that dark shelter. "Pard," he ejaculated, "he's paid. By Gawd, he's shot himself—the only good thing he's done on this trek. Squares him with me."

No man ever again looked upon the face of Eric Dann. The agony of his last moment after the confession of the deceit which plunged his brother and the drovers into tragic catastrophe was cloaked in the blanket thrown over him. An hour after the deed which was great in proportion to his weakness, he lay in his grave. Sterl helped dig it by the light of a torch which Friday held.

They were called to a late supper. Bill, actuated by a strange sentiment at variance with his abandonment of the trek, excelled himself on this last meal. The leader did not attend it.

No orders to guard the mob were issued that night. But Sterl heard Bligh tell his men they would share their last watch. The girls, wide-eyed and sleepless, haunted the bright fire. They did not want to be alone. Sterl and Red sought their own tent.

"Hard lines, pard," said Red, with a sigh, as he lay down. "It's turrible to worry over other people. But mebbe this steel trap on our gizzards will loosen now that Eric at last made a clean job of it. You never can tell about what a man will do. An' as for a woman—didn't yore heart jest flop over when Beryl answered her dad?''

"Red, it sure did."

"Bingham, we break camp at once," said Stanley Dann as he met Slyter at breakfast. "What do you say to trekking west along this river?"

"I say good-o," replied the drover. "Why not divide the load on the second dray? There's room on the wagons. That dray is worn out. Leave it here."

"I agree," returned the leader. Already the tremendous incentive of starting a new trek, in the right direction, had seized upon them all.

"My wife can drive my wagon. So can Leslie, where it's not overrough. We'll be shy of drovers, Stanley."

"Plenty bad black fella close up," Friday broke in.

Rollie tramped up to report that the mob was still resting, but that the larger herd of horses had been scattered.

"We found one horse speared and cut up. Abo work," added Rollie.

"Could these savages prefer horseflesh to beef?" queried Dann, incredulous.

"Some tribes do, I've been told. Bligh heard blacks early this morning," asserted Slyter. "We cannot get away any too soon now."

Bligh and his three dissenters drove a string of horses across the river. Bill, the cook, had slipped down the bank, under cover of the brush, to straddle one of the horses. Bligh did not say good-by nor look back but followed the drovers down the path, and into the river.

"Queer deal that," spoke up the ever vigilant Red, who sat by the fire oiling his rifle. "Bligh was sweet on Beryl at first. You'd reckon he'd say good-by and good luck to her, if not the old man."

"Red, I'll bet you two bits Bligh comes back."

"Gosh, I hope he does. I jest feel sorry for him, as I shore do for the other geezers who got turribly stuck on Beryl Dann . . ."

"Uh—oh" warned Sterl, too late.

Beryl had passed Red, to hear the last of his scornful remark to Sterl.

"You're sorry for whom, Red Krehl?"

"Beryl, I was sorry for Bligh," drawled Red, cooly. "Me an' Sterl air gamblin' on his sayin' good-by to you. I'm bettin' thet if he's smart he won't try. Sterl bets he will."

"And if Bligh's smart, *why* won't he try to say good-by to me?" retorted Beryl.

"Wal, he'll get froze for his pains."

"He will, indeed—the coward. And now what about the other geezers who're stuck on Beryl Dann?"

"Aw, just natoorally I feel sorry for them."

"Why—Why? You all-of-a-sudden noble person," she flashed, furiously.

"Wal, Miss Dann, it so happens thet I'm one of them unfortunate geezers who got turribly stuck on you," returned the cowboy.

All in one moment, Beryl was transformed from a desperately hurt woman, passionately furious, to one amazed, bluntly told the truth she had yearned for and ever doubted, robbed at once of all her blaze, to be left pale as pearl.

"Mr. Krehl, it's a pity—you never told me," she cried. "Perhaps the geezer who's so terribly stuck on me might have found out he's not really so unfortunate, after all."

"Come out of it, kids," whispered Sterl. "Here comes Bligh, and I win the bet."

The young drover faced Sterl to remove his sombrero and bow. Water dripped off him from the waist down.

"Beryl, I dislike to go—like this," he said huskily. "But when I came on this trek I had hope—of—of—of you know what. I pray your Dad gets safely through—and I wish you happiness. If it is as we—we all guess, then the best man has won."

"Oh, Bob, how sweet of you," cried Beryl, radiantly, and all the pride and scorn of her were as if they had never been. "I'm sorry for all—that you must go. . . . Kiss me good-by." And giving him her hands she leaned to him and lifted a scarlet face. Bligh kissed her heartily, but not on her lips. Then releasing her he turned to Sterl and Red.

"Hazelton, Krehl, it's been dinkum to know you," he said, extending his hand. "Good-by and good luck." Then Bligh espied Dann coming from his wagon, and strode to intercept him. At that instant Red leaped like a panther. "Injuns!" he yelled. "Duck."

Sterl ducked, his swift gaze taking the direction of Red's leveling rifle. He was in time to see a naked savage on the ridge in the very action of throwing a spear. Then Red's rifle cracked. The abo fell back out of sight on the ridge.

Sterl heard, too, almost simultaneously, the chucking thud of a spear entering flesh. Wheeling, he saw the long shaft quivering in the middle of Bligh's broad back.

"Get down behind something" yelled Sterl, at the top of his lungs. And he ran for the rifle leaning against a wagon wheel.

"Plenty black fella close up," panted Friday, and pointed to the low rise of brushy ground just back of camp.

Red's rifle cracked again. There was a hideous screech of agony. Dann and Slyter had taken refuge behind Slyter's wagon. A drover was hurrying the women inside it. "Lie down," Slyter commanded. "Stanley, here's one of my rifles. . . . Watch sharp. Along that bit of bush."

Yells of alarm from the drovers across the river drew from Dann a booming order: "Stay over there. Ride. Abo attack."

Sterl swept his glance around in search of Red. It passed over Bligh, who was lying on his side, in a last convulsive writhing.

"Pard," shouted Red, from behind the dray a dozen steps away, "they sneaked on us from the left. They'll work back that way. An' I seen Larry an' Ben ridin' hell bent for the river bank. We'll heah them open the ball pronto. . ."

Red's rifle spoke ringingly. "Ha. These abos ain't so careful as redskins."

"Where's Rollie?"

"To my right heah, back of thet log. But he's

only got his six-gun. Pard, put yore hat on somethin' an' stick it up, same as old times."

The ruse drew whistling spears. One struck the wagon seat; the other pierced Sterl's hat and jerked it away.

Again Red shot. "I got that bird, pard. Seen him throw. Aw, no, these blacks cain't throw a spear at all."

Then the drovers across the river entered the engagement, and Larry and Benson began to shoot.

"They must be slopin', pard, but I cain't see any," called Red.

The firing ceased. One of the drovers across the river hailed Dann: "They broke and ran. A hundred or so."

"Which way?"

"Back over the downs."

"You drovers get on," yelled Dann. "Clear out. Bligh's done for."

Friday appeared, darting from tree to tree, and disappeared. Red came running to join Sterl. "All over 'most before it started," he said. "Did you bore one, pard?"

"I'm afraid not. But I made one yell."

"Wal, I made up for thet. They was great tall fellers, Sterl, an' not black at all. Kinda a cross between brown an' yaller."

Presently Friday strode back into camp, his arms full of spears and wommeras. The cowboys met him, and Slyter and Dann followed in haste. Rollie was next to arrive.

"Black fella run alonga dere," said Friday. "All

afraid guns. Come back bimeby."

Red gazed down at the dead drover. "My Gawd, ain't thet tough? Jest a second quicker an' I'd've saved him. I saw somethin' out of the corner of my eye. Too late."

"Bligh stepped in front of me in time to save my life," rolled Dann, tragically. "That black was after me. Friday, will those abos track us?" queried Dann.

"Might be. Pretty cheeky."

"Pack. Hazelton, you and Krehl go with Larry and Benson. Drove the mob up the river. We'll follow behind the horses. Slyter, you and Friday help me bury this poor fellow."

Riding out with the drovers, the cowboys had a look at the dead aborigines. The savage who had murdered Bligh lay in the grass on the open ridge where Red had espied him. The abo did not resemble Friday in any particular. He was taller, more slender, more marvelously formed. The color appeared to be a cast between brown and red. His visage was brutish and wild, scarcely human. Red was wrathful over the fine horse the abos had slaughtered and cut up. "Hoss-meat eaters. When there was live beef an' daid beef for the takin'."

The mob had moved up river of its own volition. The drovers caught up in short order. The ground on this side of the river made better going than that on the other. The surface was hard and level, the grass luxuriant, the clumps of brushland widened away to the north. The sky was black with circling, drooping birds of prey. The larger gum trees were white with birds. Ahead of the mob, kangaroos dotted the rippling downs.

Friday, trotting along beside Sterl's horse, spears and wommera in hand, often gazed back over his shoulder. It was not possible to believe they had seen the last of this strange and warlike tribe of aborigines. According to Slyter, a daylight attack was extremely rare. The earliest dawn hour had always been the most favorable for the blacks to attack and perhaps the worst for the drovers, since tired guards are likely to fall asleep.

Toward sundown Slyter left his wife to drive his wagon and, mounting a horse, rode ahead, obviously to pick a camp site. Besides grass, water and firewood, there was now imperative need of a camp which the aborigines could not approach under cover. Sunset had come when Slyter finally called a halt. Three gum trees marked the spot. Off toward the river a hundred rods grew a dense copse fringed by isolated bushes. The rest was level, grassy downs.

"From now on everyone does two men's work," boomed Dann. "Mrs. Slyter and the girls take charge of rations and cooking. We men will supply firewood, and wash dishes."

"It's important to sleep away from the fire and the wagons," asserted Slyter. "Keep a fire burning all night. Blacks often spear men while they are asleep."

"Old stuff for me an' Sterl, boss," drawled Red. "We're used to sleepin' with one eye open. An' heah—why, we can heah a grasshopper scratch his nose."

But none of the trekkers laughed any more, nor

smiled.

The cowboys helped Dann and Slyter carry ground cloths, blankets and nets over to the fringe of brush near the copse. That appeared to be an impenetrable thorny brake, a favorable place, thought Sterl. Beds were laid under the brush. The three women were to sleep between Dann and Slyter. The greedy mosquitoes had become a secondary trial.

The men returned to the fire.

"It will be bright moonlight presently," Dann said. "That's in our favor. Benson, take Larry and Roland on guard. I needn't tell you to be vigilant. Stay off your horses unless there's a rush, or something unusual. Come in after midnight to wake Hazelton and Krehl."

"Hazelton, where will you sleep?" asked Benson.

"What do you say, Red?" returned Sterl.

"Somewhere pretty close to these trees, on the side away from the open. We'll heah you when you call."

When a gentle hand fell on his shoulder and Friday's voice followed, Sterl felt that he had not had his eyes closed longer than a moment.

"All well, Friday?" he asked.

"Eberytink good. But bimeby bad," replied the black.

Red had sat up, putting on the coat he had used for a pillow. Everything was wet with dew. The moon had soared beyond the zenith and blazed down with supernatural whiteness. The downs resembled a snowy range. A ghastly stillness reigned over the wildness. Even the mosquitoes had gone.

At the camp fire the three drovers whom they were to relieve sat drinking tea.

"How was tricks, Ben?" asked Red.

"Mob bedded down. Horses quiet. Not a move. Not a sound." They passed the two herds of horses, the larger of which, Dann's, were grouped between the cattle and the camp.

Red chose a position near a single tree on that side from which they could see both the mob and the remuda. They remained on foot. Friday made off into the ghostly brightness, returned to squat under the tree. His silence seemed encouraging.

"Let's take turns dozin'," suggested Red, and proceeded to put that idea into execution.

Sterl marked a gradual slanting of the moon and a diminishing of the radiance. He fell into a half slumber. When he awakened the moon was far down and weird. The hour before dawn was close at hand.

"Pard, there's no change in the herd, but Dann's hosses have worked off a bit, an' Slyter's air almost in camp," said Red.

"Ssh," hissed the black. If he had heard anything, he did not indicate what or whence. Rifles in hands, the cowboys stood motionlessly in the shadows of the tree. Several times Friday laid his ear to the ground, an action remarkably similar to that of Indian scouts they had worked with. The gray gloom made the camp fire fade into a ghostly flicker.

"Smellum black fella," whispered Friday suddenly. Like a hound, his keenest sense was in his nose. An aborigine himself, he smelled the approach of his species on the downs.

"What do?" whispered Sterl, hoarsely, leaning to Friday's ear.

"Tinkit more better along here."

"Pard, I cain't smell a damn thing," whispered Red.

"I'm glad I can't. If we could—these abos would be close . . . Red, it's far worse to stand than a Comanche stalk."

"Ssh." The black added a hand to his caution. Again the cowboys became statues.

"Obber dere," whispered Friday. And to Sterl's great relief, he pointed away from camp. But though Sterl strained his ears to the extent of pain he could not hear a sound.

Suddenly the sinister silence broke to thuds of hooves. Sterl jerked up as if galvanized.

"Skeered hoss. But not bad. Reckon he got a scent, like Friday," whispered Red.

Another little run of hooves on soft ground.

"I heahed a hoss nicker," whispered Red, intensely. Friday held up his hand. Events were about to break, and Sterl greeted the face with a release of tension.

Whang. On the still air sped a strange sound, familiar, though Sterl could not identify it. Instantly there followed the peculiar thud of missile entering flesh. It could not have been a bullet, for no report followed. Hard on that sound came the shrill, horrid unearthly scream of a horse in mortal agony. A pounding of hooves—and a heavy body thudding the ground. The herd took fright, snorting and whistling.

"You savvy wommera?" asked Friday, in a whisper.

"I shore did. An' you bet I shivered in my boots," replied Red.

Then the strange sound, almost a twang, became clear to Sterl's mind.

"Black fella spearum hoss," added Friday.

Red broke into curses. "They're cuttin' up one of our hosses . . . I can heah the rip of hide. Let's sneak over an' shoot the gizzards out of them."

Sterl gave grim acquiescence to Red's bold suggestion. But Friday whispered: "More better black fella go alonga bush corroboree."

"Pard, he talks sense," said Red. "It's better we let the abos gorge themselves on horse meat, than for us to run the littlest risk."

"Righto, Red. But it galls me," rejoined Sterl, and lapsed into silence again. New, faint sounds reached their ears—what must have been a rending of bones. Splashing sounds succeeded; and then the keenest listening was in vain. At daylight Red said he would ride out and see what signs the marauding abos might have left. Sterl returned to camp.

All the men were up and Slyter was helping his wife get breakfast. His eyes questioned Sterl in mute anxiety. But upon hearing Sterl's report he was far from mute. Dann, too, ground his teeth.

"We could spare a bullock, but a good horse—"

"Boss," said Red, as he rode into camp, "I found where them abos had killed an' butchered yore hoss. Nary hide nor hair nor hoof left. Must have been a hundred abos in thet outfit."

For ten nights that band of aborigines, reinforced at every camp, hung on the tracks of the trekkers. Nothing was ever seen of them but their haunting smoke magic. The silence, the mystery, the inevitable attack on the horses in the gray dawn, wore increasingly upon the drovers. The savages never killed a beef. The horrible fear they impressed upon the pursued was that when they tired of horseflesh they would try to obtain human flesh. For Slyter averred that they were cannibals. Friday, when anyone mentioned this dire possibility, looked blank.

Now the trekkers approached the end of the downs. The river had diminished to a creek. Day by day the patches and fringes of bush had encroached more upon the green, shining monotony. Vague blue tracery of higher ground hung over the horizon. The waterfowl, except for cranes and egrets, had given way to a variable and colorful parrot life.

"Makes no difference if we do pass the happy huntin' ground of this breed of abos," said Red, one night. "We'll only run into more. This heah bunch has got me buffaloed. You cain't see them. A coupla more hosses butchered will put me on the warpath, boss or no boss. I figger that killin' some of them would stop their doggin' us. Thet used to be the case with the plains redskins."

As the bush encroached more upon the downs,

corroborees were held nightly by the aborigines. The wild revels and the weird chantings murdered sleep for the trekkers. Always over them hovered the evil portent of what the cannibals had been known to do in the remote Australian wilderness.

One gray morning dawned with bad news for the Slyters. Leslie's thoroughbred, a gray roan stallion of great promise, which the girl called Lord Chester, was missing from the band. Red ran across the spot where he had been killed and butchered. Upon their return to camp, Leslie was waiting in distress.

"Les, we cain't find him," confessed Red. "An' I jest reckon he's gone the way of so many of Dann's hosses." She broke down and wept bitterly.

"Say, cain't you take yore medicine?" queried Red, always prone to hide his softer side under a cloak of bitterness or scorn. "This heah trek ain't no circus parade. What's another hoss, even if he is one of yore thoroughbreds?"

"Red Krehl," she cried in passionate amazement at his callousness, "I've lost horses—but Chester. It's too much—I loved him—almost as I do—Jane."

"Shore you did. I felt thet way once over a hoss. It's tough. But don't be a baby."

"Baby? I'm no baby, Red Krehl. It's Dann and Dad—and you—all of you who've lost your nerve. If you and Sterl—and Larry and Rol—if you had any man in you—you'd kill these abos."

The girl's passion, her rich voice stinging with scorn, appeared to lash the cowboy.

"By gosh, Leslie," he replied, "I shore deserved thet. No excuse for me, or any of us, unless we're jest plain worn to a frazzle."

"Red Krehl, what do you mean by that speech?" demanded Beryl.

"Never mind what I meant. Leslie hit me one below the belt."

"That is no reason for you to concoct some blood reprisal of revenge. Leslie is a grand girl. She has proved that to me. But she's like you—a savage. She forgets."

"Yeah? Forgets what?" drawled the cowboy.

"That her loss was only a horse. If you and Sterl and Larry and Rollie should be killed or badly wounded—our trek is doomed."

"Beryl," returned Red, "you're smarter than any of us. But Leslie's ravin' is more sense than yore intelligence. It's a hard nut to crack . . ."

A hundred times that day Sterl saw Red turn in his saddle to look for the smoke signals of the aborigines rising above the bush horizon to the north. Toward noon of that day they vanished. But that night in camp, when Larry, Rollie and Benson were about to go out on guard, Friday held up his hand.

"Corroboree." They listened. From the darkness wailed a chant as of lost souls.

"How far away, Friday?" asked Red, tersely.

"Close up."

"How many?"

"Plenty black fella. No gin. No lubra."

Red swept a blue-fire glance all around to see that he would not be overheard by the women.

"Fellers, it's a hunch. Grab yore rifles an' extra cartridges. We'll give these abos a mess of lead."

Friday led the way beyond camp. As they neared the bush the chant swelled to a pitch indicating many voices. Soon, dark, dancing forms grotesquely crossed the firelight. Friday led a zigzag way through the bush and brush.

They were halted by a stream or pond.

"About as far as we can get," whispered Red. "Let's take a peep. Careful now."

Silently the five rose from behind the fringe of brush, to peer over the top. Sterl was surprised to see a wide stretch of water, mirroring three fires and fantastic figures of abos dancing in strange gyrations. The distance was about a hundred yards.

"Plenty black fella," whispered Friday, in tense excitement. "Big corroboree. Full debbil along hoss meat. Bimeby bad."

"It sounds plum dangerous," whispered Red. "Mebbe he means that hossflesh has gone stale. They want long-pig. Let's frame it thet way."

"It's a cinch they'll roast us next," said Sterl.

"All right," whispered Red, tensely. "Make shore of yore first shot. Then empty your rifles pronto, reload, an' slope. Pard Sterl, forget your Injun-lovin' weakness, an' shoot like you would if one of us was in there roastin' on the coals."

They cocked and raised their rifles. Sterl drew down upon a dense group of dark figures, huddled together, swaying in unison.

"One—two—three—shoot," hissed Red.

The rifles cracked. Pandemonium broke loose.

The abos knocked against each other in their mad rush. And a merciless fire poured into them. When Sterl paused to reload he peered through the smoke. Red was still shooting. From the circle of light, gliding black forms vanished. But around the fires lay prone abos, and many writhing, and shrieking.

"Slope—fellers," ordered Red, huskily, and then turned away on the run. At length the cowboy halted from exhaustion.

"Reckon we're out of—reach of—them spears," he gasped. "I ain't used—to runnin'— Wal, did it work?"

"Work? It was a—massacre," declared Benson, in hoarse, broken accents.

"Let's rustle—for camp," added Red. "They'll all be—scared stiff."

His premonition had ample vindication. When Red called out they all appeared from under the wagon.

"What the hell?" boomed Dann, as he stalked out, rifle in hand.

"Were you attacked?" queried Slyter, sharply.

Beryl ran straight into Red, to throw her arms around him, then sink limply upon his breast. She was beyond thinking of what her actions betrayed.

"Boss," he said, "we went after them. It jest had to be done."

"Well, what happened?" demanded the leader, his breath whistling.

"We blasted hell out of them," declared Benson. "And it was a good thing."

"Hazelton, are you dumb?" queried Slyter, testily.

"Wholesale murder, boss," replied Sterl. "But justifiable. Friday intimated that we might be roasting next on their spits."

"Oh, Red," cried Beryl. "I thought you had—broken your promise—that you might be—"

"Umpumm, Beryl," returned Red, visibly moved, as he released himself and steadied her on her feet. "We was shore crazy, but took no chances. Beryl, you an' Leslie can feel shore thet bunch of abos won't hound us again."

Red's prediction turned out to be true. There were no more raids on the horses—no more smoke signals on the horizon. But days had to pass before the drovers believed in their deliverance.

They trekked off the downs into mulga and spinifex country, covered with good grass, fairly well watered and dotted with dwarf gums and fig and pandanus trees. The ground was gradually rising. They came next into a region of ant hills. Many a field of these queer earthen habitations had they passed through. But this one gave unparalleled and remarkable evidence of the fecundity and energy of the wood and leaf-eating ants. Gray and yellow in the sunlight, hills were of every size, up to the height of three tall men. At night they shone ghostly in the starlight. Sterl found that every dead log he cut into was only a shell—that the interior had been eaten away. And from every dead branch or tree poured forth an army of ants, furious at the invasion of their homes.

At last Sterl understood the reason for Australia's magnificent eucalyptus trees. In the ages past, nature had developed the gum tree with its many variations, all secreting eucalyptus oil, as defensive a characteristic as the spines on a cactus.

Then they camped on a range of low hills, with a watercourse which gave them an easy grade. Followed to its source, that stream led to a divide. Water here ran toward the west. That was such a tremendous circumstance, so significant in its power to stir almost dead hopes, that Dann called a halt to rest, to recuperate, to make much needed repairs.

"It is that unknown country beyond outback Australia," exclaimed Slyter.

Friday made a slow gesture which seemed symbolic of the infinite. Indeed this abyss resembled the void of the sky. The early morning was hot, clear, windless. Beneath and beyond him rolled what seemed a thousand leagues of green-patched, white-striped slope, leading down, down to a nothingness that seemed to flaunt a changeless inhospitality in the face of man. It was the other half of the world. It dreamed and brooded under the hot sun. On and on forever it spread and sloped and waved away into infinitude.

"Never-never land," gasped Slyter.

"White fella go alonga dere nebber come back," said Friday.

Turning away from that spectacle, the men returned down the hill. At camp Slyter reported simply and truthfully that the trek had passed on to the border of the Never-never Land. No need to repeat the aborigine's warning.

"Good-o," boomed Stanley Dann. "The Promised Land at last. Roll along, you trekkers."

Midsummer caught Dann's trek out in the arid interior. They knew it was midsummer by the heat and drought, but in no other way, for Dann and Sterl had long since tired of recording labor, misery, fight and death.

They had followed a stream bed for weeks. Here and there, miles apart, they found clear pools in rocky places. The bleached grass had grown scant, but it was nutritious. If the cattle could drink every day or two they would survive. But many of the weak dropped by the wayside. Cows with newly born calves had been driven from the waterholes; and when the calves failed the mothers refused to leave them. Some mornings the trek would be held up because of strayed horses. Some were lost. Dann would not spare the time to track them. The heat was growing intense.

The trek had become almost chaotic when the drovers reached a zone where rock formations held a succession of pools of clear water including one that amounted to a pond.

"Manna in the wilderness," sang out Stanley Dann, joyfully. "We will camp here until the rains come again."

To the girls that meant survival. To the drovers it was exceedingly joyous news. The water was a saving factor, just in the nick of time. For everywhere were evidences of a long cessation of rain in these parts. In good seasons the stream must have been a fair little river, and during flood time it had spread all over the flat. Birds and animals had apparently deserted the locality. The grass was bleached white; plants had been burned sere by the sun; trees appeared to be withering.

Dann said philosophically to Slyter: "We have water enough and meat and salt enough to exist here for five years." That showed his trend of thought. Sterl heard Slyter reply that the supply of water would not last half as long as that. "We'll have to build a strong brush roof over that pond, in case the dust storms begin," he added.

The most welcome feature of this camp was the cessation of haste. For days and weeks and months the drovers had been working beyond their strength. Here they could make up for that. The horses and cattle, after a long dry trek, would not leave this sweet water. Very little guarding would they need.

Sterl and Red, helped by Friday, leisurely set about selecting a site, pitching their tent, making things comfortable for a long stay. Working at these tasks took up the whole first day. Everyone else had been busy likewise. At supper Sterl gazed around to appreciate a homelike camp. But if, or when, it grew windy in this open desert, he imagined, they would have more to endure than even the scorching heat of the camp at the forks.

Mrs. Slyter laid out the same old food and drink, but almost unrecognizable because of her skill in cooking and serving. As for Beryl and Leslie, Red summed it up: "Wal, doggone it, I reckon a cowboy could stand a grubline forever with two such pretty waitressess . . . Heah you air, girls, thin as bean poles an' burned brown as autumn leaves."

"We're not as thin as bean poles," asserted Leslie. This epithet of Red's was not wholly true—yet how slim and frail Beryl was, and how slender the once sturdy Leslie.

The womenfolk, having served the supper, joined the drovers at the table. Afterward Larry and Rollie cleared away and washed the dishes. The drovers sat and smoked awhile, conversing desultorily.

"No flies or mosquitoes here," said Dann.

"Flies will come by and by," replied Slyter. "There'll be a good few calves dropped here."

"And colts foaled, too. But we have lost so many."

"Boss, where do you figger we air?" asked Red.

"Somewhere out in the Never-never Land. Five hundred miles outback, more or less."

"Dann, I'll catch up with my journal now," interposed Sterl. "I can recall main events, but not dates."

"Small matter now. Keep on with your journal, if you choose. But I—I don't care to recall things. No one would ever believe we endured so much. And I would not want to discourage future drovers."

Red puffed a cloud of smoke to hide his face, while he drawled: "Girls, you're gonna be old maids shore as shore can be, if we ever get out alive."

"You bet we are, Red Krehl, if help for such calamity ever depended on Yankee blighters we know," cried Leslie, with spirit.

Beryl's response was surprising and significant.

"We are old maids now, Leslie dear," she murmured, dreamily. "I remember how I used to wonder about that. And to—to pine for a husband. . . . But it doesn't seem to matter now."

"But it would be well if we could."

Stanley Dann said: "God gave us thoughts and vocal powers, but we use them, often, uselessly and foolishly. You young people express too many silly ideas . . . You girls are not going to be old maids, nor are you cowboys ever going to be old bachelors. We are going through."

"Shore we air, boss," flashed Red. "But if we all could forget—an' face this hell like you—an' also be silly an' funny once in a while, we'd go through a damn sight better."

Dann slapped his knee with a great broad hand. "Right-o. I deserve the rebuke—I am too obsessed—too self-centered. But I do appreciate what I owe you all. Relax, if you can. Forget. Play jokes. Have fun. Make love, God bless you."

As Dann stamped away, Sterl remarked that there was gray in the gold over his temples—that his frame was not so upright and magnificent as it had once been. And that saddened Sterl. How all the dead must haunt him.

The abrupt change from excessive labor, from sleeplessness and fear to rest, ease, and a sense of safety, reacted on all the trekkers. They had one brief spell of exquisite tranquility before the void shut down on them with its limitless horizon lines, its invisible confines, its heat by day, its appalling solitude by night, its sense that this raw nature had to be fought.

Nothing happened, however, that for the time being justified such fortification of soul and body. If the sun grew imperceptibly hotter, that could be gauged only by the touch of bare flesh upon metal. The scarcity of living creatures of the wild grew to be an absolute barrenness, so far as the trekkers knew. A gum tree blossomed all scarlet one morning, and the girls announced that to be Christmas Day. Sterl and Red found the last of the gifts they had brought on the trek. At supper presentations followed. The result was not in Sterl's or Red's calculations. From vociferous delight Beryl fell to hysterical weeping, which even Red could not assuage. And Leslie ate so much of the stale candy that she grew ill.

One day Friday sighted smoke signals on the horizon. "Black fellas close up," he said.

At once the camp was plunged into despair. Dann ordered fortifications thrown up on two sides. Then Friday called the leader's attention to a strange procession filing in from the desert. Human beings that did not appear human. They came on, halted, edged closer and closer, halted again, paralyzed with fear yet driven by stronger impulse. First came a score or less of males, excessively thin, gaunt, black as ebony and practically naked. They all carried spears, but appeared the opposite of formidable. The gins were monstrosities. There were only a few lubras, scarcely less hideous than the gins. A troop of naked children hung back behind them, wild as wild beasts, ragged of head, pot-bellied.

Friday advanced to meet them. Sterl heard his

voice, as well as low replies. But sign language predominated in that brief conference. The black came running back.

"Black fella starbbin deff," he announced. "Plenty sit down die. Tinkit good feedum."

"Oh, God, indeed Friday," boomed Dann, gladly. "Go tell them white men friends."

"By jove," ejaculated Slyter. "Poor starved wretches. We have crippled cattle that it will be just as well to slaughter."

Benson had butchered a steer that day, only a haunch had been brought to camp. The rest hung on a branch of a tree a little way from camp down the river course. Head, entrails, hide and legs still lay on the rocks, ready to be burned or buried. Dann instructed Friday to lead the aborigines to the meat. They gave the camp a wide, fearful berth. Slyter brought a small bag of salt. Larry and Rollie built a line of fires. Sterl and Red, with the girls, went close enough to see distinctly. The abos watched the drovers with ravenous eyes. Larry pointed to a knife and cleaver on a log. All of them expected a corroboree. But this tribe of abos had passed beyond ceremony. They did not, however, act like a pack of wolves. One tall black, possibly a leader, began to hack up the beef into pieces and, pass them out. The abo's sat down to devour the beef, raw. When presently the blacks attacked the entrails Beryl and Leslie fled.

When darkness fell the little campfires flickered under the trees, and dark forms crossed them, but there was no sound, no chant. Next day discovered the fact that the abos had devoured the entire carcass, and lay around under the trees asleep. More abos arrived that morning as famished as the first ones.

Friday had some information to impart that night. These aborigines had for two years of drought been a vanishing race. The birds and beasts, the snakes and lizards, had all departed beyond the hills to a lake where this weak tribe dared not go because they would be eaten by giant men of their own color. Friday said that the old abos expected the rains to come after a season of wind and dust storms.

The drovers took that last information with dismay, and appealed to their black man for some grain of hope.

"Blow dust like hellum bimeby," he ejaculated, solemnly.

Days passed, growing uncomfortably hot during the noon hours, when the trekkers kept to their shelters.

The aborigines turned out to be good people. Day after day the men went out to hunt game, and the gins to dig weeds and roots. Dann supplied them with meat and the scraps from the camp table. Presently it became manifest that they had recovered and were faring well. The suspicion of the drovers that they might reward good deeds with evil thefts had so far been wholly unjustified. They never came into the encampment.

One night the sharp-eyed Leslie called attention to a dim circle around the moon. Next morning the sun arose overcast, with a peculiar red haze.

A light wind, the very first at that camp which

had been named Rock Pools by Leslie, sprang up to fan the hot faces of the anxious watchers, and presently came laden with fine invisible particles and a dry, pungent odor of dust.

"Any of you folks ever been in a dust or sand storm?" asked Red Krehl, at breakfast.

The general experience in that line had been negative, and information meager. "Bushwhackers have told me that dust-storms in the outback were uncomfortable," vouched Slyter.

"Wal, I'd say they'd be hell on wheels. This heah country is open, flat an' dry for a thousand miles."

"Are they frequent on your western ranges?" queried Dann.

From the cowboys there followed a long dissertation, with anecdotes, on the dust and sandstorms which, in season, were the bane of cattle drives in their own American Southwest.

"Boys, I've never heard that we had anything similar to your storms here in Australia," said Dann, when they had finished.

"Wal boss, I'll bet you two bits—one bob—you have wuss than ours," drawled Red.

Without more ado Sterl and Red put into execution a plan they had previously decided upon. They emptied their tent and repitched it on the lee side of Slyter's big wagon. Then while they were covering the wheels as a windbreak, Beryl and Leslie approached, very curious.

"Red, why this noble look on your sweaty brow?" asked Beryl.

"Don't be funny, Beryl Dann. This heah is one hell of a sacrifice. Dig up all yore belongin's an' yore beds, an' put them in this tent."

"Why?" queried Beryl, incredulously.

"Cause you're gonna bunk in heah an' stay in heah till this comin' dust storm is over."

"Yeah? Who says so?"

"I do. An' young woman, when I'm mad I'm quite capable of usin' force."

"I'll just love that. But it's one of your bluffs."

Beryl stood before Red in her slim boy's garb, hands on her hips, her fair head to one side, her purple eyes full of defiance and something else, fascinating as it was unfathomable.

"I'll muss yore nice clothes all up," insisted Red. "But they got to go in this tent an' so do you."

"Red Krehl, you are a tyrant. I'm trained to be meek and submissive, but I'm not your slave yet."

"You bet you're not an' you never will be," said Red, hot instead of cool. "You meek an' submissive?—My Gawd."

"Red, I could be both," she returned sweetly.

"Yeah? Wal, it jest wouldn't be natural. Beryl, listen heah." Red evidently had reached to this situation with an inspiration. "I'm doin' this for yore sake. Yore face, Beryl—that lovely gold skin of yores, smooth as satin, an' jest lovely. A dry dust storm will shrivel it up into wrinkles. You girls will have to stay in heah while the dust blows. All day long. At night it usually quiets down—at

178

least where I come from . . . Please now, Beryl."

"All for my good looks," murmured Beryl, with great, dubious eyes upon him. "Red, I'm afraid I don't care so much about them as I used to."

"But I care," rejoined Red.

"Then I'll obey you," she said. "You are very sweet to me. And I'm a cat."

The cowboys helped the girls move their beds, blankets, and heavy pieces into the tent. For their own protection they packed their belongings under the wagon, then folded and tied canvas all around it, and weighted down the edges. They advised the drovers to do likewise for which advice was followed. Sterl, going to the rock pool for water, saw that the abos were erecting little windbreaks and shelters.

There seemed to be fine invisible fire embers in a wind that had perceptibly strengthened. Transparent smoke appeared to be rising up over the sun. A dry, acrid odor, a fragrance of eucalyptus and a pungence of dust, seemed to stick in the nostrils.

"There she comes, pard, rollin' along," drawled the Texan, pointing northeast, over the low ground where the bleached stream bed meandered.

At first, Sterl saw a rolling, tumbling, mushrooming cloud, rather white than gray in color, moving toward them over the land. With incredible speed it blotted out the sun, spread gloom over the earth, bore down in convolutions. Like smoke expelled with tremendous force the front bellied and bulged and billowed, whirling upon itself, and threw out great round masses of white streaked by yellow, like colossal roses.

They ran back to camp, aware of thick streams of dust racing ahead of them. They wet two sheets and fastened one over the door of the girls' tent.

"Air you in there, girls?" shouted Red.

"Yes, our lords and masters, we're here. What's that roar?" replied Beryl.

"It's the storm, an' a humdinger. Don't forget when the dust seeps in bad to breathe through wet silk handkerchiefs. If you haven't handkerchiefs use some of them folderol silk things of Beryl's thet I seen once."

"Well, you hear that, Leslie? Red Krehl, I'll wager you have seen a good deal that you shouldn't have."

"Shore, Beryl. Turrible bad for me, too. Adios now, for I have no idee how long."

Sterl's last glimpse, as he crawled under the wagon, was the striated, bulging front of the dust cloud, almost upon them.

"And now to wait it out," he said, with a sigh as he lay down on his bed. "We have a lot to be thankful for. Suppose we were out in it?"

"Suppose thet mob rushes? There wouldn't be no sense in goin' out to stop them."

They settled down to endure. It was pretty hot inside. After awhile invisible dust penetrated the pores and cracks in the canvas. Red had covered his face with a wet scarf, and Sterl followed suit. After sunset the wind lulled. The cowboys went out. An opaque gloom cloaked the scene. The dust was settling. The drovers were astir; the Slyters getting supper.

By evening the air had cleared a good deal and cooled off. After supper, Sterl and Red went out with the drovers to look for the horses and cattle. They had not strayed, but Dann ordered guard duty that night in three shifts. When they returned, Friday sat by the fire with a meat bone in one hand and a piece of damper in the other.

"How long storm last?" asked Red.

"Old black fella say bery long."

"Friday, I wish the hell you'd be wrong once in awhile," complained Red.

"Bimeby," said the black.

Sterl kept a smooth-barked piece of eucalyptus in his tent, and for every day that the dust blew and the heat grew more intense he cut a notch. And then one day he forgot, and another he did not care, and after that he thought it was no use to keep track of anything because everybody was going to be smothered.

Yet they still carried on. Just when one of the trekkers was going to give up trying to breathe the wind would lull for a night. Every morsel they ate gritted on the teeth. The drover nightly circled the mob and horses; and butchered a bullock now and then for themselves and the abos. Fortunately their drinking water remained pure and cool, which was the one factor that kept them from utter despair.

Leslie, being the youngest, and singularly resistant in spirit, stood the ordeal longest before beginning to go downhill. But Beryl seemed to be dying. On clear nights they carried her out of the tent, and laid her on a stretcher. At last only Red could get her to eat. Sterl considered it marvelous that she had not passed away long ago. But how tenaciously she had clung to love and life. Red had become silent, grim, in his grief over Beryl.

One night, after a scorching day that had been only intermittently windy, the air cleared enough to let a wan spectral moon shine down upon the camp. There was a difference in the atmosphere which Sterl imagined to be only another lying mirage of his brain. Friday pointed up at the strange moon with its almost indistinguishable ring, and said: "Bimeby."

In the pale moonlight Beryl lay on her stretcher, a shadow of her old self, her dark little face lighted by luminous lovely eyes that must have seen into the infinite. She was conscious. Dann, in his indestructible faith, knelt beside her to pray. Red sat at her head while the others moved to and fro, silently like ghosts.

"Red—don't take it so hard," whispered Beryl, almost inaudibly.

"Beryl—don't give up—don't fade away," implored Red, huskily.

"Red—you'd never—marry me—because of. . . ."

"No. But not because of thet. . . . I'm not good enough to wipe your feet."

"You are as great—as my Dad."

Sterl led the weeping Leslie away. He could endure no more himself. Red would keep vigil beside Beryl until she breathed her last. He had no feeling left when he put the clinging Leslie from him and slunk back to his prison under the wagon, to crawl in like an animal that hid in the thicket to die. And he fell asleep.

He awoke in the night. The moan of wind, the rustle of leaves, the swish of branches were strangely absent. The stillness, the blackness, were like death.

Then he heard a faint almost imperceptible pattering upon the canvas. Oh, that lying trick of his fantasy. That phantom memory of trail nights on the home ranges, when he lay snug under canvas to hear the patter of sleet, of snow, of rain. He had dreamed of it, here in this accursed Never-never Land.

But he heard the jingle of spurs outside, and the soft pad of Friday's bare feet.

"Pard—Pard. Wake—up."

That was Red's voice, broken, sobbing.

"It's rainin'—pard—Beryl's gonna live."

For nineteen days it rained—at first steadily. Before half that time was over the dry stream bed was a little river running swiftly. After the steadiest downpour had ceased, the rains continued part of every day and every night. On the morning of the twentieth day since the dust storm, the drovers arose to greet the sun again, and a gloriously changed land.

"On with the trek," boomed Stanley Dann.

He gave the aborigines a bullock, and steel implements that could be spared. When the trek moved out of Rock Pools these black people, no longer scarecrows, lined up stolidly to watch the white men pass out of their lives. But it was impossible not to believe them grateful.

The grass waved green and abundant, knee-high to a horse; flowers born of the rain bloomed everywhere, gum trees burst into scarlet flame, and the wattles turned gold; kangaroos and emus appeared in troops upon the plains. Water lay in league-wide lakes, with the luxuriant grass standing fresh and succulent out of it. Streams ran bank-full and clear, with flowers and flags bending over the water.

The Never-never Land stretched out on all sides, boundlessly. It was level bushland, barren in dry seasons, rich now after the rains. Eternal spring might have dwelt there.

Only the black man Friday could tell how the trekkers ever reached the oasis from the camp where Beryl came so near dying in the dust storm and his limited vocabulary did not permit of detailed description.

"Many moons," repeated the black perplexedly. "Come along dere." And he pointed east and drew a line on the ground, very long, very irregular. "No black fella, no kangaroo, no goanna. This fella country no good. Plenty sun. Hot like hell. White fella tinkit he dies. Boss an' Redhead fightum. Cattle no drink fall down. Plenty hosses go. White fella sit down. No water. Friday find water. One day two day alonga dis I'm waterbag. Go back. Makeum come."

That was a long dissertation for the black. Sterl

pieced it together and filled in the interstices. His mind seemed to be a labyrinthine maze of vague pictures and sensations made up of hot sun and arid wastes, of wheels rolling, rolling, rolling on, of camps all the same, of ghostly mirages, the infernal monotony of distances, and finally fading faces, fading voices.

He had come to his senses in a stream of clear, cool running water. Gray stone ledges towered to the blue sky. There were green pastures, full-foliaged trees blossoming gold, and birds in noisy flocks. Once more the melodious cur-ra-wong of the magpie pealed in his dulled ears.

"God and our black man have delivered us once more. Let us pray instead of think what has passed," said Stanley Dann, through thick, split lips from which the blood ran. All seemed said in that.

As great a miracle as the lucky star that had guided the trekkers here was their recovery through sweet fresh cool water. Even its music seemed healing. It gurgled and bubbled from under the ledges to unite and form a goodly stream that sang away through the trees to the west. That was the birth of a river which ran toward the Indian Ocean. For Sterl, and surely all of them, it was the rebirth of hope, of life, of the sense of beauty. On the second morning Leslie staggered up to gaze about, thin as a wafer. She cried: "Oh, how lovely. Paradise Oasis."

Beryl could not walk unaided, but she shared Leslie's joy. How frail a body now housed this chastened soul. Hammocks were strung for them in the shade, and they lay back on pillows, wide-eyed.

Wild berries and fruit, fresh meat and fish, bread from the last sack of flour, added their wholesome nourishment to the magic of the sweet crystal water.

"Let me stay here forever," pleaded Beryl.

And Leslie added: "Oh, Sterl, let us never leave."

One morning Friday sought out Sterl. "Boss, come alonga me."

"What see, Friday?" queried Sterl.

The black tapped his broad breast with his virile hand. "Black fella tinkit see Kimberleys."

"My—God," gasped Sterl, suddenly pierced through with vibrating thrills. "Take me."

They scaled a gray escarpment. Far across a warm and colorful plain an upflung purple range rolled and billowed along the western horizon.

Turning toward camp and looking down, Sterl cupped his hands and loosed a stentorial yell that pealed in echo from hill to hill. He waved his sombrero. The girls waved something white in return. Then Sterl ran down the hill, distancing the barefooted black.

Leslie ran to meet him, her heart in her eyes. But Sterl saved his speech for that gaunt, golden-bearded leader. The moment was so great that he heard his voice as a whisper.

Ten days down the stream from that unforgettable Paradise Oasis the trek came out of a bushland into more open plains where rocks and trees and washes were remarkable for their scarcity. The trekkers had been reduced to a ration of meat and salt with one cup of tea, and one of stewed dried fruit each day. They throve and gathered strength upon it, but Sterl felt certain that the reaction came as much from the looming purple range, beckoning them on. Twenty-two hundred strong, the mob had improved since they struck good water, and every day calves were born, as well as colts. No smoke signals on the horizon.

One day Sterl rested a lame foot by leaving his saddle for Slyter's driver seat. Slyter's good wife lay asleep back under the canvas, her worn face betraying the trouble that her will and spirit had hidden while she was awake. Sterl talked to Slyter about the Kimberleys, the finding of suitable stations, the settling, all of which led up to what was in his mind—the future.

"Slyter, would it interest you to learn something about me?" asked Sterl.

"Indeed it would, if you wish to tell," returned the drover.

"Thanks, boss. It's only that I'd feel freer—and happier if you knew," rejoined Sterl, and told Slyter why he and Red had come to Australia.

"And we'll never go back," he concluded.

"After this awful trek, you can't still like Australia."

"I'm mad about it, Slyter."

"You tell me your story because of Leslie?"

"Yes, mostly. But if there had been no Leslie, probably I'd have told you anyhow."

"She loves you."

"Yes. And I love her, too. Only I have never

told her that nor the story you've just heard."

"Sterl, I could ask little more of the future than to give my daughter to such a man as you, or Krehl. We have been through the fire together. . . . As for you, young man, Australia will take you to its heart, and the past will be as if it had never been."

"I'm happy and fortunate to be able to cast my lot with you."

"Righto. And here comes sharp-eyed Leslie. Sterl, I think I'll get off and straddle a horse for awhile. You drive and talk to Leslie."

Almost before the heavy-footed drover was on the ground, Leslie was out of her saddle to throw him her bridle reins.

"How jolly," she cried in gay voice, as she leaped to a seat beside Sterl. "Months, isn't it, Sterl, since I rode beside you like this?"

"Years, I think."

"Oh, that long long agony—but I'm forgetting it. Sterl, what were you talking to Dad about? Both of you so serious."

"I was telling him what made me an outcast—drove me to Australia."

"Outcast? Oh, Sterl. I always wondered. Red, too, was so strange. But I don't care what you've ever been in the past. It's what you are that—that made me. . . ."

When she hushed up, Sterl repeated the story of his life and its futility.

"How terrible. Sterl, was—was Nan very pretty? Did you love her very much?"

"I'm afraid so."

"Love is a terrible thing."

"Les, that gives me an idee, as Red says. Let's get the best of this old terrible love."

"Sterl, it can't be done. I know."

"Les, it can. Listen. You get hold of Red the very first chance—tonight in camp. Tell him that Beryl is dying of love of him—that she dreams of him—babbles in her sleep—that she can't live without him. . . . And anything more you can make up."

"Sterl Hazelton, I wouldn't have to lie. That is all absolutely true," returned Leslie.

"You don't say? That bad? Then all the better. Leslie, I'll tell Beryl what a state Red is in over her."

"Is it true? Does Red care that much?" queried Leslie.

"Yes. I don't think it's possible to exaggerate Red's love for that girl. But he feels he is a no-good cowboy, as he calls it."

"You bet I'll help," she flashed. "But—but who is going to—to tell *you* about *me*?"

"Oh, that? Well, darling, if you think it's necessary you can tell me yourself."

She fell against him, quivering, her eyelids closed. He wrapped his arm round her and drew her close. At this juncture Mrs. Slyter's voice came to them wildly.

"I've been listening to some very interesting conversation."

"Oh—Mum," faltered Leslie, aghast, starting up.

But Sterl held her all the closer. Presently he

said: "Well, then—Mum—we have your blessing, or you would have interrupted long ago."

Sterl had contrived to get Red and the girls for a walk along the stream, and there at a murmuring waterfall, he led Beryl away from their companions.

"I'm terribly fond of you, Beryl."

"I am of you, too, Sterl. But you—and Red will be leaving us to become wanderers again—seeking adventure. I wish I were a man."

"Who told you we'd be doing that?"

"Red."

They paused beside a rock, upon which Sterl lifted Beryl to a seat, and he leaned against it to face her.

"So that geezer has been hurting you again? Dog-gone him. Beryl, I'm going to double-cross him, give him away."

"You mean betray him? Don't, Sterl."

"Ummpumm. We're not—leaving," he said. "I wouldn't leave Leslie and. . . ."

"Oh, Sterl. Then—then—"

"Yes, then. And Red would never leave me. For why?" Here Sterl related for the third time that day the story of his exile.

"How wonderful of Red. Sterl, this Aussie lass will make up for all you've lost."

"Beryl, I'd be happier than I ever was if you and Red . . . "

"If only he could see," she interrupted, passionately. "If only he could forgive and forget Ormiston—what I—what he . . . "

Sterl grasped her slim shoulders and drew her

down until her face was close.

"Hush. Don't say that—don't ever think of that again," he said, sternly. "That is absolutely the only obstacle between you. The jealous fool in his bad hours thinks you regret. . . . I won't say it, Beryl Dann. And for Red's sake and your and ours, Les's and mine, forget. Forget. Because Red Krehl worships you. Don't grieve another single hour. Don't believe in his indifference. Break down his armor. Oh, child, a woman can, you know. Why—why Beryl. . . ."

She slid off the rock into his arms, blind, weeping, torn asunder, her slender hands clutching him. "No—more," she sobbed. "You break—my heart—with joy. I—I had—despaired. Twice I have—nearly died. I knew—the next time . . . But this—this will save me."

Day after day the purple range loomed closer. The scouts saw at last that the stream they had followed for so long was presently going to join a river. That green and gold line disappeared round the northern end of the range. And the next day the leader of the drovers, for once actuated by haste, made for the junction. Blue smoke rose about the big trees. It must come from aboriginals, but it was not hostile.

"Boss, I ben tinkit no black fella," said Friday to Sterl.

Sterl rode ahead to tell Dann.

"Aye, my boy, I guessed that," he cried. "We have fought the good fight. With His guidance. Look around you, Sterl—richest, finest land I ever saw. Ha. A road—a ford," and Dann pointed. He had indeed come to a road that sloped down under the giant trees to the shallow stream. His followers all saw, but none could believe his eyes.

Three white men came out into the open, halting to stare. The pointed. They gesticulated. They saw Dann's wagons, the women on the drivers' seats, the mounted drovers, the big band of horses, the great mob and ran to meet the trekkers. Dann halted his four horses, and Slyter stopped beside him. The mounted drovers line up, a lean ragged crew with Leslie conspicuous among them, unmistakably a girl, bronzed and beautiful.

"Good day, cobbers," called Dann.

"Who may you be?" replied one of the three, a stalwart man with clean-shaven, rugged face and keen, intelligent eyes.

"Are those mountains the Kimberleys?" asked Dann, intensely.

"Yes. The eastern Kimberleys. Drover, you can't be Stanley Dann?"

"It really seems I can't be. But I am," declared Dann.

"Great Scott. Dann was lost two years and more ago, according to reports at Darwin. It has taken you two years and five months to get here."

"But death visited and dogged our trek, alas," said Dann. We trekked almost to the Gulf and then across the Never-never Land. And we lost several drovers, five thousand head of cattle, and a hundred horses on the way."

"My word. What great news for western Australia. I see you have a mob of cattle left. I'm glad to be the first to tell you good news."

"Good news?" boomed Dann, in echo.

"Well, rather. Dann, cattle are worth unheard of prices. Horses the same. Reason is that gold has been discovered in the Kimberleys."

"Gold."

"Yes, gold. There's been a rush-in for months. Mines south of here. Trekkers coming in from Perth and Fremantle. Settlers by ship to Darwin and Wyndham. I have been freighting supplies in to the gold fields. My name is Horton."

"Do you hear, all?" boomed Dann. "The beginning of the empire I envisioned."

"We all hear, Stanley, and our hearts are full," replied Slyter.

"What river is this?" queried Dann, shaking off his bedazzlement to point to the shining water through the trees.

"That is the Ord. You have come down the Elivre," replied Horton. "Dennison Plains are in sight to the south. The finest country, the finest grazing for stock in the world."

"Aye, friend. It looks so. But this road? Where does it lead and how far?"

"Follows the Ord to the seaport, Wynhdam, a good few miles less than two hundred. You are in the nick of time, Dann. The government will sell this land to you so cheap it is unbelievable."

"Ha. This land?" called Dann, his voice rolling. "Dann's Station. This will be our range."

"Stanley, we must send at once for supplies," said Slyter, rousing.

"Horton, do we look like starving trekkers?"

"Indeed you do. I never saw such a peak-faced,

ragamuffin lot of drovers. Or ladies so charming despite all."

"They have lived for days now wholly on meat."

"Forgive me, Dann, for not thinking of that. Sam, run and boil the billy. Dann, I can let you have tea, fruit, sugar, tinned milk. . . ."

"Enough, man. Do not overwhelm us. Slyter, what shall we do next—that is, after that cup of tea?"

"Stanley, we should thank heaven, pitch camp, and plan to send both wagons to Wyndham for supplies."

"Wal, air you gonna ask us to get down an' come in?" drawled Red. "I reckon I can stand tea."

"American," called out Horton, with twinkling eyes.

"Savvied again. The name is Krehl. An' heah's my pard, Hazelton."

After supper, Beryl and Leslie went into conference over the innumberable things they wanted bought. Sterl and Red sat beside a box and racked their brains to think of necessities to purchase from town.

"Strange, Red, just think," ejaculated Sterl. "we don't really need anything. We have lost the sense of need."

"Yeah. How about toothbrushes, powder, soap, towels, iodine, glycerine, combs, shears to cut hair—an' socks?"

"On account of the girls we must get over all these savage habits, I suppose. . . . Have you made up your mind about Beryl?" Sterl asked, averting his eyes.

"Pard, she cared more about me than I deserve—than I ever had a girl care for me before. An' lately—I don't—know how long she's been diffcrent. All that misery gone. She's forgot Ormiston an' every damn bit of thet—thet.... An' she's been happy. Jest the sweetest, softest, lovingest, most unselfish creature under the sun. An' I'd be loco if I didn't see it's because of me— that she takes it for granted...."

"I should think you'd be the happiest man in the world," declared Sterl, feelingly. "I am."

"I reckon I'd be too, if I'd jest give up."

"Red—right this minute—do it."

"Holy mackeli, don't knock me down. All right, old pard, I knuckle, I show yellow. But there's a queer twist in my mind. She always got the best of me. If I could jest think up one more way to get the best of her before, or mebbe better when I tell her how I want her—then I'd match you for who's the luckiest an' happiest man." He changed the subject abruptly. "Have you looked over this range? Grandest I ever seen. Wal, think. I've got more money in my kick than I ever earned in my life. An' you had a small fortune when I seen yore belt last."

"I have it all, packed in my bag."

"Good. Wal, bright prospect, huh?"

By the eighth day, on which Benson and Roland were expected to return with the wagons and supplies, Sterl and Red had progressed well with their cabin building. The site was the Ord River side of the wooded point, high up on a grassy, flower-spangled bank, shaded by great trees from the morning sun, and facing the Kimberleys.

The cabin was to have thatched roof and walls, for which Friday scouted out a wide-leaved palm, perhaps a species of pandanus. Slyter designed the framework, which consisted of long round poles carefully fitted. Larry, who was a good carpenter, often lent a helping hand. The girls, enthusiastic over its beauty, visited the site several times a day. Red, who was now unusually mild and sweet, made one characteristic remark.

"Say, anybody would think you girls expected to live over heah with us fellers."

That sally precipitated blushes, a rout, and from a little distance, very audible giggles.

"Red, that was a dig," remonstrated Sterl. "You are a mean cuss. If you would only take a tumble to yourself the girls could come over here to live."

"Hell. I've shore tumbled. What do you want for two bits? Canary birds? An' why don't you figger out thet trick for me to play on Beryl? I cain't last much longer. Why, when she comes near me I go plumb loco."

"Whoopee. That's talking. I've got the deal planned."

"Yeah?"

"It's clever. Even Dann thought so. He agreed. And he was tickled."

"You double-crossin' two faced, Arizonie geezer," ejaculated Red. "You told Dann before you told me?"

"Sure. I had to get his consent. Listen, pard. . . ."

Excited cries broke in upon their colloquy. The girls appeared off at the edge of the grove. Leslie cupped her hands to her lips and shrieked: "Boys, wagon's back. Come."

They raced like boys, to draw up abreast and panting before two bulging, canvas-covered wagons, and their excited comrades.

"Mr. Dann," Benson was saying. "Ten days going and coming. Fair to middling road. One wagon loaded with food supplies, milk, sugar, vegetables, fruit, everything. Other full of personal articles. . . . Four freight wagons following us with lumber, galvanized iron roofing, tools, utensils, hardware, harness, mattresses, staples—the biggest order ever filled in Wyndham."

While the big wagons were being unpacked, while the cowboys whooped and the girls squealed, a steady, voluminous stream of questions poured into the bewildered ears of Benson and Roland, who had been to town, to a seaport, who had heard news of the world, and of the old home.

Gold had indeed been discovered in the south and west of the Kimberleys. Ships and prospectors, sheepmen and drovers, trekkers and adventurers were coming forth from Perth and Fremantle and points far to the south. Ships plied regularly to Darwin. Stanley Dann's trek across the Nevernever Land was the wonder of two busy seaports.

There were letters for all the company except

Sterl and Red. Somehow that silenced the drawling Red and struck a pang to Sterl's heart. Stanley Dann read aloud in his booming voice a communication from Heald. He had got out safely with his comrades and the mob of cattle Dann had given them. They worked out toward the coast into fine grazing country where he and his partners established a station. Ormiston's three escaping bushrangers had been murdered by aborigines. A rumor that Dann's trekkers had perished on the Never-never had preceded Heald's return to Queensland. But he never credited it and chanced a letter. The government had offered to sell hundred-mile-square tracts of land in the outback for what seemed little money.

"Gosh. A hundred-mile square ranch," drawled Red. "I reckon I gotta buy myself a couple of them."

They settled themselves in the pleasant shade. Mrs. Slyter and Leslie served tea. Beryl sat pensive and abstracted. On that auspicious morning, when all had been gay, Red had not deigned to give her even a smile. What a capital actor Dann was. To all save Sterl and Red he appeared only the great leader, glad and beaming.

Presently Dann produced a little black book, worn of back and yellow of leaf. He opened it meditatively.

"Beryl, will you please come here," he said, casually. "In this new and unsettled country I think I may be useful in other ways besides being a cattleman. I shall need practice to acquire a seemly dignity, and clarity of voice."

He continued to mull over the yellow pages. Sterl saw the big fingers quiver ever so slightly. Beryl, used to her father's moods, came obediently to stand before him.

"What, Dad?" she inquired, curiously.

"Sterl, come here and stand up with Beryl," he called. "No, let Krehl come. He might be more fitting."

Red strolled forward, his spurs jingling, his demeanor as cool and nonchalant as it ever had been.

"I've observed you holding my daughter's hand a good few times on this trek," Dann said, mildly. "Please take her hand now."

As Red reached for Beryl's hand she looked up at him with a wondering smile and her color deepened. Than Dann stood up to lift his head and expose his bronze-gold face, which appeared a profound mask, except for the golden lightning in his amber eyes.

"What's the idea, boss?" drawled Red.

"Yes, Dad, what is all this?" faltered Beryl, confused.

"Listen, child, and you, Krehl," replied Dann. "This should be fun for you, and surely for the others. Please watch me. Criticize my ministerial manner and voice. Trekking does not improve even the civilized and necessary graces. Well, here we are. . . ."

And in a swift resonant voice he ran over the opening passages of the marriage service. Then, more slowly and impressively, he addressed Red.

"James Krehl, do you take this woman to be your lawful wedded wife. . . . to have and to hold.

. . . to love and to cherish . . . until death do you part?"

"I do," replied Red, ringingly.

The leader turned to his daughter. "Beryl Dann, do you take this man to be your lawful wedded husband. . . . to have and to hold. . . . to love, cherish and obey until death do you part?"

"I—I—I do," gasped Beryl, faintly.

Dann added sonorously: "I pronounce you man and wife. Whom God has joined together let no man put asunder."

Beryl stared up at him, visibly prey to conflicting tides of emotions. It had been a play, of course, but the mere recital of the vows, the counterfeit solemnity, had torn her serenity asunder. When her father embraced her, thick-voiced and loving, she appeared futher bewildered.

"Daddy, what a—a strange thing—for you to practice that on me."

"Beryl, it is the most beautiful thing of the ages. . . . Krehl, I congratulate you with all my heart. I feel that she is safe at last."

Sterl dragged the astounded and backward Leslie up to the couple. "Red, old pard, put it there," he cried, wringing Red's free hand. "Beryl, let me be the first to kiss the bride." Leslie could only stare, her lips wide.

"But—but it was only a play," flashed Beryl. Then Red kissed her lips with a passion of tenderness and violence commingled.

"Wal, wife, it was about time," drawled Red.

That word unstrung Beryl. "Wife?" she echoed, almost inaudibly. "Red. You—you married me—really? Father. Have I been made a fool of?'' cried Beryl, tragically.

"My daughter, compose yourself," returned Dann. "We thought to have a little fun at your expense. I am still an ordained clergyman. But you are Mrs. Krehl. I'll have marriage certificates somewhere in my luggage."

She swayed back to Red. She could not stand without support. She lifted frail brown hands that could not cling to Red's sleeves.

"Red. You never asked me."

"Wal, honey, the fact was I didn't have the nerve. So Sterl an' I went to yore Dad an' fixed it up. Beryl, he's one grand guy." He snatched the swaying girl to his breast. Her eyelids had fallen.

"Beryl," he shouted, in fear and remorse. "Don't you dare faint. Not heah an' now of all times in our lives. I did it thet way because I've always been dyin' of love for you. Since thet—thet orful time I've been shore you cared for me, but I never risked you outwittin' me. I swore I'd fool you onct an' go on my knees to you the rest of my life."

Suddenly she was shot through and through with revivified life. She did not see any others there. And when she lifted her lips to Red's, it was something—the look of both of them then—that dimmed Sterl's eyes.

"Come, Sterl and Leslie," boomed Dann. "I require more practice. Here, before me, and join hands. Our bride and groom there may stand as witnesses." And almost before Sterl was sensible of anything except the shy and bedazzled girl beside him, clutching his hand, he was married.

Friday wrung Sterl's hand. No intelligence could have exaggerated what shone in his eyes.

"Me stopum alonga you an' missy. Me be good black fella. No home, no fadder, no mudder, no brudder, no lubra. I'm stay along you, boss."

Sterl and Red walked by the river alone.

"Pard, it's done," said Red. "We're Australians. Who would ever have thunk it? But it's great. All for two no-good gunslingin' cowboys."

"Red, it is almost too wonderful to be true."

It was as Stanley Dann had said of them all: "We have fought the good fight." In that moment Sterl saw with marvelous clarity. It had taken a far country and an incomparable adventure with hardy souls to make men out of two wild cowboys.

Springfield .45-70
John Reese

Price: $1.95 0-505-51789-2
Category: Western

Madman with a Mad Gun

Raitt was a killer with a big grudge against the world. Now he was out to get repaid for his suffering. First he'd kill rancher Mike Banterman and steal the payroll money. With his .45-70 he figured there'd be no stopping him. Power, women, money—his for the taking!

Three Complete Western Novels:

Gun Brat
Wes Yancey

Breed Blood
Ben Jefferson

A Renegade Rides
Lee Floren

Price: $2.75 0-505-51788-4
Category: Western

Triple Western

Three action-packed, rip-roaring adventure classics, by three of the greatest Western writers ever to tame the wild frontier!

Fargo #9: The Sharpshooters

John Benteen

Price: $1.75 0-505-51790-6
Category: Western

One-Man Feud

The Canfield clan, thirty strong, had left their North Carolina mountains and were raising hell in Texas. When one of them killed a Texas Ranger, the lawmen sent Fargo in to root out the killer. The Rangers wanted no quarrel with the Canfields, but they figured Fargo was tough enough to hold his own against the entire clan.

PRICE: $1.95 0-505-51802-3
CATEGORY: Western

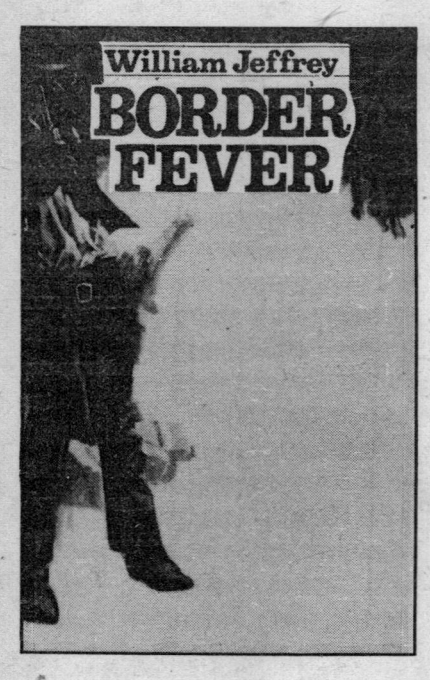

BORDER FEVER

William Jeffrey

A hardened and worldwise Arizonan, Ranger Oak M'Candliss was also a loner. His brothers had been massacred during a Chiricahuas border raid and the wife he adored had been murdered by a pack of vicious outlaws. All he had left was a devotion to justice and a determination to uphold the law.

FARGO #8 Valley of Skulls

The golden gun

A party of scientists digging around an ancient Mayan temple was trapped in the hottest corner of a bloody Mexican revolution. The country was crawling with bandits, the kind of men who would kill you for no more than an old pair of boots.

Fargo was hired to bring out the scientists, along with a beautiful woman and a legendary golden Spanish cannon.

John Benteen

PRICE: $1.95
0-505-51803-1

CATEGORY: Western

SEND TO: TOWER BOOKS
P.O. Box 511, Murray Hill Station
New York, N.Y. 10156-0511

PLEASE SEND ME THE FOLLOWING TITLES:

Quantity   Book Number   Price

IN THE EVENT THAT WE ARE OUT OF STOCK
ON ANY OF YOUR SELECTIONS, PLEASE LIST
ALTERNATE TITLES BELOW:

Postage/Handling
I enclose .....

FOR U.S. ORDERS, add 75¢ for the first book and 25¢ for each additional book to cover cost of postage and handling. Buy five or more copies and we will pay for shipping. Sorry, no. C.O.D.'s.

FOR ORDERS SENT OUTSIDE THE U.S.A., add $1.00 for the first book and 50¢ for each additional book. PAY BY foreign draft or money order drawn on a U.S. bank, payable in U.S. ($) dollars.

☐ Please send me a free catalog.

NAME _____
(Please print)

ADDRESS _____

CITY _____ **STATE** _____ **ZIP** _____
Allow Four Weeks for Delivery